Garth held out the fur. "Let's start, Miranda."

She was suddenly awed by the momentousness of what they were about to do.

"There are three steps." Garth's tone was even and controlled. "First, rub the herb potion all over your body."

Bracing herself against the strange sensation, she began covering her arms, her neck, and her face with the brown concoction. Before long her skin began to tingle. Her flesh actually seemed to be absorbing the potion.

The mixture affected her mind, as well.

"Garth," she said breathlessly, "I feel strange."

"Miranda!" He grasped her shoulders. "It's not too late to go back."

"No," she insisted. "I want to go forward."

He hesitated. Then he lifted the heavy wolfskin up onto her shoulders. "This is the second step."

She leaned forward as he spread it out across her back. The animal fur was heavy, much more so than she'd expected.

"Are you sure you can manage?" he asked.

"Yes. I have to." The sound of her own voice startled her. It sounded so far away.

The forest was swirling around her. She was having trouble focusing on what was happening. And so she simply gave in to it, putting herself in Garth's hands.

Don't miss these exciting books
from HarperPaperbacks!

Dark Moon Legacy
Volume I   *The Curse*
Volume II   *The Seduction*
Volume III   *The Rebellion**

Read these other terrifying thrillers

Sweetheart
Running Scared
by Kate Daniel

Dead Girls Can't Scream
by Janice Harrell

Deadly Stranger
by M. C. Sumner

* coming soon

DARK MOON Legacy

VOLUME II

The SEDUCTION

CYNTHIA BLAIR

HarperPaperbacks
A Division of HarperCollinsPublishers

This is a work of fiction. The characters, incidents, and dialogues are products of the author's imagination and are not to be construed as real. Any resemblance to actual events or persons, living or dead, is entirely coincidental.

HarperPaperbacks *A Division of* HarperCollins*Publishers*
10 East 53rd Street, New York, N.Y. 10022

Copyright © 1993 by Daniel Weiss Associates, Inc., and Cynthia Blair
Cover art copyright © 1993 Daniel Weiss Associates, Inc.

All rights reserved. No part of this book may be used or reproduced in any manner whatsoever without written permission of the publisher, except in the case of brief quotations embodied in critical articles and reviews. For information address Daniel Weiss Associates, Inc., 33 West 17th Street, New York, New York 10011.

Produced by Daniel Weiss Associates, Inc., 33 West 17th Street, New York, New York 10011.

First printing: November, 1993

Printed in the United States of America

HarperPaperbacks and colophon are trademarks of HarperCollins*Publishers*

10 9 8 7 6 5 4 3 2 1

VOLUME II

The SEDUCTION

CHAPTER
1

Miranda sat at the edge of the lake, gazing down at the young man whose head was cradled in her arms. Tenderly she ran her fingers through his tousle of thick blond curls. As he looked up at her, his blue eyes were pleading. "Miranda, I don't know how you can bear to look at me."

She studied his face, illuminated by the pale light of dawn. The transformation from beast to man was nearly complete. All traces of the animal he had become under the full moon were vanishing as a new day streaked the blue-gray November sky with fiery oranges and vibrant pinks. Gone were the powerful jaws, the pointed nose, the sharp ears, the sleek golden fur. In their place were the handsome features of the shy, quiet boy named Garth Gautier who had appeared so suddenly and so mysteriously in this small village on the craggy Oregon coast.

His body had also been reshaped. His chest was still massive, his shoulders and arms sinewy, his legs long and muscular. Yet this was the body of a man, not a bestial night hunter who raced through the forest beneath the full moon, stalking his prey.

He reached up, gently stroking Miranda's cheek. "Now that you know me for what I really am," he said, his voice soft yet edged with fear, "can you still love me?"

Miranda blinked away the tears welling up in her eyes. It was true; now she did know him for what he really was.

Werewolf.

She knew what the word meant. She'd heard the legends. A werewolf was an uncontrollable beast. An evil being driven by a diabolical force. A supernatural creature forced to shapeshift from man to animal every twenty-nine days, whenever the moon was full.

A monster.

Yet Garth Gautier was no monster. She had lost her heart to him the first time she'd seen him. Standing in the Overlook Public Library, hidden by the towering shelves of books, she had spotted him—and fallen in love.

Now that you know me for what I really am, can you still love me?

Miranda replayed the scene of the night before over again in her mind. She and her best friend, Elinor Clay, had been on their way home from the Overlook Playhouse where Miranda had just triumphed as the lead in the play *Saint Joan*. The two girls were walking along the edge of the forest, their way lit by the full moon, when from out of the woods sprang a wild animal.

It was huge, larger than any ordinary wolf. Its muscular torso was nearly six feet long, its head so large it could easily crush any living thing with its oversize jaws.

What had struck Miranda even more than its massive size was its color. Its fur was unlike that of any wolf she'd ever seen: a rich shade of gold, thick and lustrous, gleaming in the moonlight.

Her immediate response had been fear. Fear, along with the powerful urge to protect Elinor. Instinctively Miranda had stepped in front of her friend, prepared to fight off the animal herself.

But the moment she'd looked into the beast's eyes, she knew. She recognized those eyes. They were filled with pain and regret, but their distinctive shade of blue was unmistakable.

And there was more. It was as if his eyes enabled her to see into his soul, acting as mirrors that reflected what was inside.

At that moment she'd finally understood.

Suddenly she knew why he had continued to fight their love. He had been trying to protect her from the knowledge of what he was. Despite her struggle to understand his resistance, regardless of how much she pleaded with him to explain, he'd maintained his silence, saying only that the secret he harbored was so terrible it meant they could never be together.

Now it all made sense.

Miranda looked up from where she was sitting—a grassy knoll at the edge of a lake nestled in the forests surrounding Overlook. She could see the two of them reflected in the calm waters. The long red velvet gown, her costume from the play, was spread out around her, the soft folds of fabric dotted with leaves and blades of grass. Her hair, a wild mane of black waves, framed her head and her bare shoulders like a halo. Her dark brown eyes had an intensity about them that contrasted with her delicate features.

Garth lay with his head in her lap, his muscular form stretched out against the uneven ground. His thick golden hair was unruly and she continued to run her hands through it, in an attempt to calm him.

In the background were the black silhouettes of trees, their gnarled branches reaching out of the undulating gray-white coils of morning mist. The sky grew lighter with every passing second, the pastels of morning driving away the deeper shades of the night.

Eagerly Miranda drank in every detail. This

was a moment she wanted to remember. One she would always treasure.

The moment of acceptance. She knew now this was a love to which she would give herself completely—without hesitancy, fear, or restraint.

She blinked away the tears that filled her eyes. There was still so much to understand. Garth's was a world she knew little about. And she sensed it was crucial she learn everything she could.

While this was an end—not only to her innocence, but also to her confusion—she recognized it was also a beginning.

Now that you know me for what I really am, can you still love me?

She understood that Garth was driven by an evil force, something outside himself, a power so terrible it was beyond her grasp. After shapeshifting into werewolf form he had viciously attacked two people, both students at Overlook High School. One of them, Andy Swensen, Miranda had known only as the class bully. The other, Corinne Davis, was a friend. True, Corinne's loyalty had recently been thrown into question, but Miranda had been close to her for more than a decade.

The consequences of these attacks had been devastating. Corinne was still in a state of delirium, unable to remember what had happened to her that night under the full moon, incapable of making contact with the world around

her. Andy had fared much worse. His attack had
been fatal.

Even now, after discovering that Garth had
been the one who had committed the attacks,
Miranda was able to accept him. Her love was so
strong that it enabled her to see him not only as
the victim of a destructive force, but also as the
man he truly was. He wasn't the one responsible
for those heinous acts. It wasn't his choice to
shapeshift into a wild beast, to change into a
night hunter . . . to kill.

The evil power was responsible.

She knew in her heart she could not blame
Garth.

All she could do was love him. Love him—
and help him fight the vile curse.

And so, gazing into his questioning eyes, she
was able to give him her answer.

"Yes, Garth," she replied. "I love you. Even
now, when I finally know you for what you are."

"Miranda." He lifted his head until their lips
met. He placed a gentle kiss on her mouth,
sweet and undemanding. She sensed it was a
kiss born of relief. "I can't believe I found
you."

She stroked his head, running her fingers
through his golden hair.

"I want us to be together," she told him in a
hoarse whisper.

"Even now?"

"Even now," she insisted. "I want to know everything. I *need* to know. Will you share your secrets with me?"

She felt his body grow tense.

"Do you know what you're asking?" he demanded.

"I know I love you. And that I want to know all there is."

"It's terrible, Miranda. I want to keep you out of it."

"I'm already in it," she said patiently, running one finger down his cheek, tracing the outline of his face. "Won't you let me all the way in?"

He hesitated. Looking into his eyes, Miranda could see his uncertainty.

And then, shining through, she saw the love.

"All right," he said simply.

Miranda and Garth walked in silence, their hands clasped together as they headed up Winding Way, a twisting dirt road that cut through the dense forests edging Overlook. All around them the new morning was driving the night away. The dark sky faded to a clear watery blue, the intense ribbons of lavender and orange and rose already fading. The moon's light grew pale as the sun peered over the horizon, casting long dark shadows over the ragged terrain.

The November morning was biting. Miranda shivered, then leaned against Garth as he wrapped his arm around her protectively. Despite the gloominess of the place, she was looking forward to taking refuge at Cedar Crest, the mansion that had been in the Gautier family for generations. For now, it was Garth's home.

As they rounded one last bend in the road, the house came into view, its top floors rising up just beyond the towering trees. Reminiscent of a European castle, it had clearly been a showplace at one time. The facade was constructed of gray stones, their pale flatness a striking contrast to the mountains surrounding it. The two main wings formed an L and were joined by a tall tower. One exterior wall was made almost entirely of French doors that looked out over a garden.

Despite its stateliness, Miranda had always found Cedar Crest cold and unwelcoming. Even as a little girl, when she and her friends had come biking around here, they'd considered getting even close to the place a daring adventure. For decades no one had lived in it. Over the years it had fallen into a deplorable state of decay, disintegrating into nothing but a dark vision looming at the end of a meandering dirt road.

The gray stones were crumbling, the brick path running from the circular driveway to the front door was covered with clumps of weeds. The windows had always reminded Miranda of hollowed-out eyes, empty black spaces that saw nothing. Many of the wooden shutters bordering them had come loose from their hinges, hanging at odd angles. In the garden, stagnant waters filled lifeless pools, thickly covered with algae. Cracks marred the hand-painted tiles that surrounded them, their once bright colors now faded.

An all-pervasive gloominess hung over this glorious mansion that had been left to die. Yet what had always struck Miranda even more was the eerie silence that surrounded the place, blanketing it like a shroud. No birds sang, no bees buzzed, no wildflowers bloomed. Instead, there was a terrible stillness, one that reminded her of death.

Even recently, when she'd come in search of Garth, that had been her impression. And so as she neared the end of Winding Way and the house came fully into view, she gasped.

Cedar Crest had been transformed.

The mansion looked fresh and vibrant. Standing proudly against the backdrop of the clear blue morning sky, Cedar Crest gave the impression of a dignified queen, bedecked in her finest, prepared for some special occasion. The gray stones were intact, the brick walkways in perfect condition, the shutters aligned with the windows. The entire house emanated warmth.

"Garth! Look!" Miranda broke free of his grasp, then ran toward the mansion to get a better look.

She stepped into the garden, her eyes darting about, taking in the magnificent changes. Even though it was a biting November day, this was a spring garden, vibrant with new life. Bright, colorful blossoms burst forth at every turn, their fragrance gently perfuming the air. Bees buzzed at the edges of petals, birds chirped their songs from the branches of fruit trees. A delightful sweetness hovered in the air.

Miranda stood in the middle, exclaiming over each discovery. When Garth came up beside her, she grasped his arm.

"Oh, Garth!" she cried. "Is this really Cedar Crest?"

"This is Cedar Crest as it was meant to be."

Glancing up at him, she saw that his face reflected the same jubilance over the mansion's transformation that she felt.

Yet he did not seem at all surprised.

"What does it mean, Garth?" she asked him. "How did this happen?"

He bent down to pick a few colorful blossoms, dark purple bluebells and yellow daffodils. Handing her the nosegay, he said simply, "Your love, Miranda."

Miranda stared at him with wide eyes.

"It's your love that's responsible. The strength of your feelings for me. The fact that you now know me for what I am—and you still love me. Your acceptance has revived Cedar Crest."

She sniffed the bouquet, her eyes locked onto his. "Take me inside. I want to see more."

Her arm linked in Garth's, she walked toward the front door. As the two of them grew near, it opened by itself, as if beckoning them inside. Miranda glanced at Garth. Once again his face registered no surprise.

When they stepped over the threshold, she cried out. Inside, as well, the house had come back to life.

The mansion consisted of more than thirty rooms, spread out over the three stories. The first floor was a maze of sitting rooms, parlors, and drawing rooms. Along one entire side of the building ran a ballroom. Upstairs, countless bedrooms flanked long, twisting corridors. Every room was ornate, decorated with handpainted murals, dense Oriental carpets, and thick velvet fabrics in rich, dark colors.

This morning, she ran from room to room, all of them once decayed but now beautiful, eagerly drinking in the magical transformation of each one. The velvet curtains that ran from the ceiling to the floor, once dull and tattered and thick with dust, were once again luxurious fabrics in rich tones: dark red, royal blue, forest green. The gold-leaf trim around the windows, formerly faded and flaking off in many spots, shone anew.

The colors in the murals scattered throughout the house were once again vibrant. The romantic scenes they depicted practically came alive: lovers with their eyes locked together, frolicking cherubs with chubby legs and rosy cheeks, clusters of serene animals congregating in peace. She took it all in, cries of joy and surprise springing from her lips at every turn.

Filled with anticipation, Miranda approached what she knew had once been the jewel of the house: the ballroom. She stepped inside, holding her breath, hopeful that here, too, there had been a magical transformation. She was not disappointed. The mirrors that entirely covered the longest wall, once cracked and yellowed, were instead as clear as crystal. The dark green marble floor, the ornate running frieze where the walls joined the ceiling, the distinctive cornices atop the windows . . . they were all magically restored.

Directly opposite the mirrors was the long row of French doors leading out to the gardens. They, too, looked brand-new. The sheer white curtains were no longer frayed at the hems. They billowed gently in the cool but gentle breeze wafting through the partially open doors.

Completely absorbed in admiring the ballroom's beauty, Miranda didn't hear Garth come in.

"Do you like it?" he asked in a soft voice, lightly placing his hand on her shoulder.

"Oh, yes!" she cried. "It's so beautiful. Garth, it's a miracle!"

"You're the miracle." He leaned over and gently kissed her, his lips warm and soft against hers. "Don't you understand, Miranda?

This is all because of your love."

He took her in his arms, pulling her close against him. He kissed her again, this time more fervently. She clung to him, her fingers gripping his powerful muscles. Being here with him felt so right. Part of her was afraid that she was simply dreaming. Yet she knew it was real—wonderfully real.

Miranda drew back. For a long time she simply gazed at him, trying to absorb his presence, luxuriating in this magnificent moment in which nothing else existed but the two of them.

"This place is magic," she finally said.

"You're magic."

"*We're* magic." She leaned forward, her lips pressing against his neck. "Look, Garth. Look at the power of our love." She placed the palms of her hands against his cheeks. His skin felt so warm, so comforting.

"There's so much I need to know," Miranda said, slipping her hand into his. "Let's go out into the garden."

Together they passed through the French doors, the silky white fabric of the billowing curtain brushing against the thick red velvet of Miranda's gown. She sat on the stone bench nestled in among the rosebushes that lined the back wall. Once scraggly and barren, they were now lush and green, covered with roses in every shade of red, yellow, pink, and white.

She reached for Garth's hand, pulling him down beside her.

"Tell me everything," she urged. "Take me back to the very beginning."

CHAPTER
2

"I—I don't know where to start."

Garth sat on the stone bench, his body rigid.
The last time he'd ventured outside, this bench
had been crumbling. Its cold gray surface was
pitted, the legs that were carved into lions' paws
worn away almost beyond recognition. Now, just
like everything else in the garden, it had been
restored to its former magnificence.

All around him, spring flowers brought the garden to life, their fragrance gently perfuming the
air, their vibrant colors splashing against their
backdrop of green like the dramatic strokes made
by a watercolor brush. Still, his interest in the magical transformation of Cedar Crest was fleeting. He
was too involved in his own ruminations. Too absorbed in remembering, in reliving his past.

Most of all, in experiencing all over again the
same excruciating torment.

He glanced over at Miranda, sitting beside him. He hoped that, somehow, he would find in her face the courage to go on. As always, he was overwhelmed by her loveliness. Her large brown eyes fixed upon him intently. Her cascade of dark wavy hair framed her sweet face like a halo. Her full mouth tensed with concern.

"I want to hear everything," she told him, her voice gentle and devoid of all judgment.

He took a deep breath. "For as long as I can remember, I felt I wasn't like everybody else. Even when I was growing up, I didn't have many friends. Sometimes I hung out with the crowd from the neighborhood, but I knew I didn't belong. Not really.

"My teachers were always telling me I was too serious. Too intense. Too self-absorbed. They sent me to the school psychologist. I suppose they thought I was depressed. Or maybe just mixed up."

He shook his head. "That wasn't it. Instead, it was as if I were carrying around a terrible secret . . . but even I didn't know what the secret was. It preyed on me constantly, driving me further and further away from everyone else."

Garth reached down and picked up a twig. He held it for a moment, studying it. Suddenly he broke it in half. "It wasn't until I turned fifteen that everything snapped into place."

"What happened then?" asked Miranda.

He gazed off in the distance, not focusing on

anything in particular but wanting to avoid looking her in the eye. "It began right after my fifteenth birthday. During that first full moon."

Garth was speaking more softly, the strain he was feeling reflected in his voice. "I can remember it all so clearly. I was alone in my room that night, studying for a math test. It was getting late. All of a sudden I started feeling strange. My skin began to prickle. It was like a thousand thorns were being stuck into my arms and legs. And every nerve in my body became hypersensitive, as if an electric current were being shot through me.

"But what was even worse was the feeling that I was losing my grip on reality. The room was fading away. I couldn't concentrate on the page in front of me. The numbers got blurry, and they ceased to mean anything to me. But at the same time, I was hearing things I'd never be able to hear normally. I could hear my parents talking downstairs, even though the door to my room was closed. I could hear the water moving through the pipes in the wall.

"At first I figured I was just tired. Nervous about the test. But then this overwhelming urge to be outdoors came over me. This was in Portland, don't forget—not exactly the wilds. But even so, I felt I was being pulled by the night. I had the bizarre sensation that the moon was drawing me toward it. And its lure was so powerful, so strong . . ."

Garth swallowed hard as he relived the scene that had taken place more than three years earlier. "The next thing I knew, I was outdoors, standing in an alley. I could hardly believe what was happening. It was like a dream. But I knew it wasn't a dream; it was real.

"The light from the full moon was so bright it was like I was standing under a spotlight. I watched as my entire body started to change. My arms got longer and thicker until they weren't arms at all, but a second set of legs. My fingernails stretched into claws. I could feel my face changing. My teeth got long and sharp, my jaw stretched, my ears became elongated. Golden hairs started sprouting all over my body."

He glanced over at Miranda. Her hands were clasped together so tightly he was certain they must be causing her pain. She didn't appear to notice. "Oh, Garth! Weren't you scared?"

"Petrified." He hesitated. "But at the same time there was something fascinating about it. It was intriguing, like something out of a movie. I managed to step outside myself and watch, not really understanding what was happening but still unable to look away.

"There was something else, too." Garth hesitated. He was aware that he was about to admit to Miranda something he had difficulty admitting even to himself. "In an odd way, it actually felt good. I mean, you can't imagine the power you feel, shapeshifting into animal form. All of a sudden, you've got strength and speed and courage unlike anything you could even imagine as a human. My senses were exaggerated. Besides being able to hear everything, I could smell things I'd never noticed before. People, animals, even the few trees that were around . . . they each had their own distinctive scent.

"Suddenly I felt bigger than life. It was like being truly *alive,* for the very first time.

"Anyway," he continued, sitting back on the bench, "there I was, a wolf. A werewolf. I spent the entire night scrounging around the garbage pails of Portland." With a hollow laugh, he added, "Not a very glamourous initiation into the enchanted world of werewolfery."

"Is that why you finally left Portland?" Miranda asked, her voice nearly a whisper. "To find a place where you could run wild in the forest?"

His muscles tensed. "No." *Should I tell her?* he wondered. *Do I dare admit to her the whole truth?*

And then, seeing the trust in her eyes, he continued.

"I left because I had to. You see, Miranda, the first full moon after I turned eighteen was the first time I killed."

She looked puzzled. "The first time you killed an animal?"

"The first time I killed a human."

He felt her stiffen beside him. He feared her shock, her disdain . . . her hatred. Yet he had come this far. He had to go on. "It was a cold night. There were few people around. I foraged for food around the city. Mostly I poked around in the alleyways behind restaurants. I'd already learned which places were best. And I had little competition. Once a stray cat or even a rat spotted me, he'd be out of there like a shot.

"But that night there was a new kind of hunger gnawing away at me. Nothing made it go away. And then I spotted a homeless man, sleeping behind a Dumpster."

Involuntarily Garth shuddered. "It was only then that I began to understand the nature of the power that ruled me. That it was something evil that caused me to shapeshift. And that even though I felt free when I was in wolf form, in the end my actions were controlled by that dark force.

"When I think of it now, I wonder I didn't end it all the very next day, as soon as I realized what I'd done. I could have gone to the police, but I knew they'd never believe me. So I ran. I knew about Cedar Crest, and even though I'd only seen pictures, I packed up my things and came down here."

"What about your parents?" asked Miranda.

Garth shook his head. "My mother never came looking for me. Maybe she knows where I am; maybe not. She does know about the family curse. She probably figures it's best simply to leave me alone."

"And your father?"

"My father disappeared a few years ago. He was a scientist who spent a lot of time in northern Canada, collecting specimens and doing research. He always lived a very solitary life, sending letters and money home but visiting only on rare occasions. For years his long absences made me angry. Now, of course, I understand."

"Garth—" Miranda began, reaching out for him.

"There's more," Garth interrupted, swallowing hard. "This power that's responsible for the shapeshifting manifests itself in other ways. Recently I've started having . . . visions."

"Visions?"

"That's right. They've come upon me suddenly. Both times were here at Cedar Crest, late at night when I was roaming around, unable to sleep."

"What kind of visions, Garth?"

He glanced over at her. Once again the urge to protect her, to keep the truth from her, had come upon him. But looking into her face, he knew he could hold nothing back.

"The first time," he said, his voice strained, "I went into the ballroom late at night. At first I thought I was dreaming. But it was so real, almost as if it were actually happening . . ."

"What, Garth? Tell me?"

"I—I could smell the smoke. I could feel her pain—"

"Whose pain?"

"Saint Joan." He closed his eyes. "I saw Joan of Arc, being burned at the stake. At least, at first. But then it changed. The scene shifted. It—it was somebody else."

"Who?"

Garth shook his head. "I don't know. The crowd was calling his name: 'Pierre Gautier.' There were people watching who cared about him. Who loved him. A woman and a little boy."

"His wife and his son," Miranda said quietly.

"Probably." Garth took a deep breath. "They burned him at the stake, just like Joan of Arc."

"Was he accused of being a heretic, of going against his church?"

"No." Garth hesitated. He remembered the scene with such clarity it seemed to be playing before him all over again. An angry mob surrounded the helpless man; his hands were tied to a wooden stake. Mercilessly the flames leapt up around him. His young face was twisted in agony, his eyes filled with terror.

From the clothes the man was wearing, Garth had a sense this scene was taking place around the same time as the burning of Joan of Arc; the Middle Ages, probably the 1400's or the 1500's. And from the language in which the angry onlookers cried out, he knew it was happening in France.

He could still hear the words of the riotous crowd: *"Pierre Gautier! Pierre Gautier!"*

And then, with even more fury, one lone voice stood out from among the rest: *"Tuez-le! Tuez le loup-garou!"*

Although he didn't speak French, he'd known instinctively what those words meant. *"Kill him! Kill the werewolf!"*

The man who was being burned at the stake had been a werewolf. He was being executed because of what he was.

Garth had understood immediately that he faced the same destiny.

He choked on his words as he told Miranda, "The man in my vision was my ancestor, Pierre Gautier. And he was burned at the stake because he was . . . like me."

"Oh, Garth!" Miranda grabbed his arm, burying her face in his shoulder. "That was centuries ago. People were fearful, they were superstitious—"

"Do you think they're any different now?" he cried. Immediately he regretted speaking to her in such an angry tone. "I'm sorry, Miranda. It's just that I'm sure he committed the same atrocities I've committed after shapeshifting. I—I've killed."

There was a long silence. It was Miranda who finally broke it, her voice so soft he scarcely heard her words. "And your other vision?"

"That one came to me as I was lying in bed, unable to sleep. It was right after I sent you away from here. After Andy Swensen's death."

He could barely bring himself to look at her. When he finally did, he saw there was nothing accusing in her eyes, no recriminations. He realized then how deep her understanding was, how complete her acceptance of the fact that the actions of the beast who roamed the forest beneath the full moon had nothing to do with Garth Gautier, the man.

"This vision was totally different. It wasn't France; it was here, along the Oregon coast. I was a werewolf—but I wasn't myself. It was another time, a time long past. I was racing through the forest, hunting. There were people around, the Native Americans who still inhabited this region when the French fur trappers first arrived. In my vision, the werewolf was racing through their settlement. It wasn't afraid of them, yet they clearly lived in fear of it."

He paused, clamping his eyes shut against the horror of the memory. "It was ruthless. It—it chose the most powerful member of the tribe as its victim—"

Garth couldn't go on. Beside him, Miranda moved closer, tightening her grip on his arm.

"These visions are your link with your past," Miranda said quietly. "I know they're torture to endure, and perhaps the evil force, the one that controls your shapeshifting, wants you to suffer. But they still hold a key."

"A key? To what?"

"To whatever it is that forces you and your family to live with this curse, generation after generation."

Garth nodded. Up until this point, he had seen those visions only as a means of torment. But Miranda was right. Perhaps if he could understand them, he could unlock the mystery. Maybe, just maybe, there was a chance. . . .

Immediately he dismissed the thought. All his life he'd been forced to live with this. Being a werewolf had kept him apart. Dictated how he lived his life. Commanded even how he felt about himself, creating an intense hatred deep inside because of the horrible crimes he'd committed.

"There's something else. Something besides the visions." This time, he blurted out what was on his mind. "A few weeks ago, I distinctly felt the presence of something . . . something *alive* in the woods. Something evil." He was shaking his head as he spoke. "It was right before you stumbled upon Andy Swensen's body. Remember? You and I were having an argument. You were saying I was holding something back from you—which I can now admit I was. You ran ahead, and I was left on my own."

He shivered at the memory. "Suddenly an evil presence was everywhere. It rose up from the ground. I heard a terrible laugh that made the whole world tremble. And I could smell death. It practically smothered me, it was so thick. But what was even worse was the feeling that a hundred hands were grabbing at me. Their fingers were . . ."

"Were like ice," Miranda finished for him, her tone one of astonishment. "I've felt it, too! I've felt the evil presence. I didn't understand it. I tried to tell myself it didn't really happen, that I just imagined it. But Garth, it sounds exactly like what you experienced."

Garth frowned, alarmed. "What happened?"

"It was the day after the Homecoming Dance. I'd spent the night at Elinor's house, and I was walking home early the next morning. I made a point of going through the woods because I was still upset about the way you ran off at the dance."

"There was a full moon that night," said Garth.

"Yes." Miranda took a deep breath. "I ran into Featherwoman in the forest."

"Featherwoman?"

"She's a Native American who lives on the edge of town. No one knows how old she is. Some people say she's a hundred. But everyone agrees that she knows everything about the lore of the tribes of the Oregon coast. I first met her when I was in elementary school. I was doing a research project on the totem pole in the middle of Overlook."

Garth smiled coldly. "The one with the wolf at the top."

"Yes." Her eyes clouded for a moment as she thought about how peculiar the hand-carved wolf head had looked to her lately. On more than one occasion it seemed to be staring straight at her, its eyes burning red, its mouth stretched into an ugly snarl. . . . Before today she'd always thought that her imagination had been playing strange tricks on her. Now, she mused, perhaps something else was responsible.

"Anyway," she went on, "I came across her walking in the woods that morning. We started talking . . . and the things she said frightened me."

"What did she say?"

"She spoke about the power of the forest. She implied that it was filled with strange forces. She made it sound as if the narnauks were not merely a legend, but that they were real."

"The narnauks?" Garth repeated.

Miranda nodded. "They're spirits. Both good and evil. The Native Americans believed they lived in nature. Featherwoman told me they're in the rocks and the trees, the sun and the moon . . . and especially in the animals. She talked a lot about the Wolf Clan."

"The Wolf Clan?" The words made Garth's blood run cold.

"Yes. The tribes around here were divided into clans. The clans' members believed they were descended from one person, someone who had ties to a supernatural being that had once appeared to him in animal form. The being gave him special powers—those possessed by the animal."

"And the clan that lived in this area was called the Wolf Clan."

"Yes. That's why there's a wolf on top of the totem pole in town. The word 'totem' means supernatural animal being, and the carvings in the wooden pole record the clan's history."

She hesitated. Garth was tempted to ask if there was something more, something she wasn't telling him.

But he simply said, "Go on."

"As Featherwoman was telling me this, I suddenly got the feeling somebody—or something—was behind me. It was then she told me about the narnauks." Nervously Miranda ran her fingers through her thick mane of dark hair. "She said they were trying to speak to me. She told me to give myself up to them."

"What did she mean?"

Miranda shook her head. "I'm not sure. But she said they were trying to warn me."

"Of what, Miranda?"

"I don't know. But I could feel them, Garth. It was just the way you said. They were grabbing me around the ankles, their fingers like ice. I was so afraid! And then . . ."

He leaned over and took her in his arms, holding her closely against him.

"I—I was wearing that Native American necklace, the same one I'd worn to the dance the night before. It's made of tiny animals hand-carved out of stone—"

"I remember it." Garth also remembered the visceral reaction he'd had to it. Just looking at it had caused his stomach to tighten with fear. "In the center there's a wolf fetish."

Miranda nodded. "All of a sudden, the wolf on the necklace got so hot it began to burn my skin. I pulled it off and threw it to the ground."

"What did Featherwoman say?"

"She didn't even seem surprised. She simply said, 'They have chosen you. You cannot avoid your fate.' It really scared me. And then she started talking about how the wolf possesses the strongest power of all the animals. She said something about a conflict between good and evil, and how both were calling to me—"

She stopped. Garth looked into her eyes, expecting to see fear. Instead, he saw only confusion.

"I didn't understand any of it, Garth. I just ran out of the woods, leaving my necklace behind. By the time I reached the edge of the forest, the strange feeling was gone. I managed to convince myself I'd imagined most of it, and that Featherwoman was just an old crazy woman who goes around trying to scare people."

"Do you still believe that, Miranda?" asked Garth.

"I wish I could." She choked on her words. "I've tried to put the whole thing out of my mind, believe me. But there were other things—"

"Yes?"

She looked him squarely in the face. "When I came out of the woods after that strange encounter with Featherwoman, I happened to glance up at the totem pole. I know it sounds crazy, Garth, but I could swear its teeth were bared and its eyes were glowing red."

She lowered her eyes. "And it was staring straight at me."

Garth simply nodded. "Go on."

"But the time I felt the narnauks most strongly was that night I found Andy Swensen's body in the woods. After we left the police station, I went back to the same spot. I wanted to try to make sense of what had happened.

"While I was there, in the spot where Andy had been killed, I felt both presences, Garth. The good and the evil. It was unmistakable. The evil one was there first. It—it was pulling on me. It had me by the ankles, and it was dragging me . . . down, down. . . .

"But then I was released. It was as if I'd been lifted upward, away from the evil power. . . . It was unlike anything I'd ever experienced before, as if I were feeling the heights of ecstasy, the depths of despair for the first time."

Garth could see the tension in Miranda's face. "But what remained with me, even stronger than the feelings, was the knowledge that something monumental is happening all around us, Garth. And that I'm a part of it."

Garth was struck by Miranda's strength and bravery. Reaching up with one hand, he touched her cheek lightly. "Miranda, my love," he said, his voice a hoarse whisper.

He leaned foward, hesitating for only a moment before pressing his lips against hers. His kiss was gentle at first, growing more and more ardent as he felt her respond. With both arms he encircled her, drawing her close against him.

Kissing her was as sweet as he had known all along it would be. His breath grew quick as with the tips of his fingers he tenderly traced the outline of her face, the graceful slope of her jaw, the softness of her neck. He felt a stirring deep inside as a brand-new passion awakened, breaking through the barriers he had kept in place for so long.

"I love you," he murmured, his lips against the fragrant skin of her throat.

At that moment, the rest of the world ceased to exist. For him, there was only Miranda.

CHAPTER
3

It was mid morning by the time Miranda made her way home. Heading down Winding Way, a wave of exhaustion suddenly hit her. She realized that she hadn't gotten any sleep since the night before last. And the thirty-six hours in between had been an incredible strain. Being in the play, discovering Garth's secret, returning with him to Cedar Crest to find the decaying mansion had undergone a magical transformation . . . suddenly her body was crying out for rest. She veered off the path, into the woods, opting for the shortcut home.

The woods were resplendent, the thick white curls of morning mist just beginning to burn off as the pale November sun rose higher and higher in the sky. The drops of dew still splattered everywhere glistened in the oblique light like so many diamonds. It was a frosty morning, the air fresh and biting. Miranda raised her hands to her cheeks and found they were icy cold.

Still, it was invigorating, trudging over the rough terrain, her steps confident as she made her way over the rocky surface of the forest floor. She braced herself as she passed over a slippery bog, using the log that lay across it as a narrow bridge. In here, where the simplest tasks required all her concentration, her worldly concerns seemed far away. Surrounded by the majestic cedars that reached up into the sky, immersed in nature in its rawest form, she found a sort of peace.

Here in the forest, even the biggest, most insurmountable problems seemed small.

Miranda paused to catch her breath, stepping out from the trees onto the ledge of one of the steeper cliffs. Looking down toward the ocean, through the clearing mist, Miranda could make out Devil's End. It was the most treacherous section of the coastline, the spot in which the rocks were particularly craggy, their ragged edges unusually sharp.

She stood gazing down for a long time, hypnotized by the sight of the waves of the Pacific crashing against the perilous coastline. Over and over again the ominous dark-green swirls hit the rocks head-on, only to burst violently into sprays of white foam. Even from so high up, the stretch of beach looked menacing. She could easily understand how sailors had chosen its nickname.

She turned away and as she did she found herself head to head with a snarling wolf, its face thrust into hers. She let out a loud gasp, more surprised than afraid. Her heart was pounding and her adrenaline pumping.

"Featherwoman!" Miranda clutched one hand against her wildly beating heart, the other hand reaching for the necklace the older woman was holding out to her. "You scared me!"

She was a small woman, her back curved with age. Featherwoman's face was leathery, her piercing black eyes sharp and wise. Some people said she was more than a hundred years old. Others claimed she had mystical powers.

Even though she barely knew her, Miranda had a special place in her heart for the old woman. In the fifth grade, she'd done a report on the totem pole looming up from the midst of Overlook, hoping that learning its history would banish her fear of it. Featherwoman had been helpful, patiently explaining the lore of her tribe to the eager ten-year-old girl Miranda had been.

Yet even as Miranda took the necklace from her with a relieved laugh, she was on guard. The last time she'd run into the mysterious woman while walking through the forest, she'd had then the same feeling she had now: that their meeting was more than coincidence.

"Thank you," Miranda said. "I thought it was—"

"You're going to need it. It is important for what is to come."

A chill ran down Miranda's spine. "Featherwoman, what are you—"

But the old woman seemed unaware of Miranda's presence. Her black eyes were closed, shut tight as if she were trying to block out something too horrible to witness.

"A terrible trial lies ahead, my child. You will need strength. You will need courage. Above all, you will need the powers of the good narnauks."

Miranda was silent. She stood frozen to the spot, unable to move. And then it happened again. Just like the last time, an incredible lightness infused her body. She felt weightless, yet at the same time extremely strong. She felt as if she could fly. A surge of energy rushed through her, a sense of power so strong she suddenly felt she could do anything.

It was like a dream. A wonderful dream, one in which there were no limits to what she could do. She was fearless, all-knowing, capable of even the most difficult and exhausting physical feat.

Yet she knew it wasn't a dream.

And then, just like the last time, the feeling vanished as suddenly as it had come.

Featherwoman opened her eyes. She reached for Miranda's arm, clasping it tightly in her gnarled fingers.

"They will help you, my child. Remember this. The forces of evil are strong and persistent. But they have a formidable foe. The good narnauks are also powerful. You must give of yourself to help them prevail."

"Give of myself?" Miranda repeated. "How? How can I give of myself?"

"You will know." Featherwoman's voice was so soft Miranda had to strain to hear. "When the time is right, you will know."

A thick curl of mist rose up, seemingly from nowhere. Miranda blinked in surprise. When she opened her eyes, Featherwoman was gone.

She looked down. Clutched in her fist was the necklace. Slowly she opened her fingers, expecting once again to be burned by the wolf charm.

Yet rather than feeling hot, the wolf charm was merely warm. It was a good kind of warmth. Tranquil. Comforting. Life-giving.

Standing in the dim light of the forest, Miranda stared at it. The black stone was giving off its own light. It glowed like coal, edged in bright orange, the dark green swirls meanwhile moving about, forming delicate patterns like the waves of the sea.

Miranda was still slightly dazed as she opened the back door of her house and stepped into the kitchen, suddenly aware that she was still in her velvet gown, the costume from the play the night before. She found her mother sitting at the kitchen table, leisurely leafing through the newspaper. The rich savory smell of a fresh pot of coffee filled the room. The brightness and warmth inside were a welcome contrast to the frigid November day.

The homey scene was a relief after the strangeness of the last twelve hours. It also reminded her she had some explaining to do about having been out all night. A dozen different excuses began forming in her head. She was shocked when her mother's face lit up into a soft smile.

"Hi, sweetie. Have fun at Elinor's last night?"

Miranda quickly rearranged her expression to something more casual. "Uh, yes."

"Good. I wasn't particularly surprised when she called last night to say you were sleeping at her house."

Thank you, Elinor! Miranda thought.

"You deserved something special, Miranda, after the wonderful performance you gave." She smiled, her pretty face youthful and calm. Since her parents' separation a few weeks earlier, Miranda hadn't seen her looking so radiant. "It was an important night for you."

By now, Miranda's performance as the lead in *Saint Joan* seemed eons away. Yet it really had been only the evening before. And she'd relished every minute. Being onstage, taking on a new persona as she transformed herself into the character of Joan of Arc . . . it had been exhilarating beyond anything Miranda had ever experienced.

Yet while it had all been very exciting, what had been at least as thrilling was the fact that Miranda's parents had come to the play together.

A scene from almost two months earlier flashed into her mind. She had come home from school one Monday in early October, gleeful over having recently learned she was one of a few high school girls invited to audition for the part of Joan of Arc in a local theater group's production of *Saint Joan*.

She'd stopped dead in her tracks when she walked into the kitchen that day and found both her parents there, their faces tense. She knew instantly something was wrong. Terribly wrong.

"Miranda, your father and I have decided to live apart for a while. It's just a trial separation. . . ."

She could still remember her mother's words as clearly as if she'd heard them only the day before.

But she pushed all that out of her mind. She concentrated instead on the image of her father and her mother coming backstage to congratulate her the evening before, right after the play— together.

"It looked to me as if last night was an important night for you, too," Miranda observed, keeping her tone light. She deposited the necklace she'd been clasping in her hand into the antique sugar bowl her mother kept on display. Then she poured herself a glass of orange juice from the pitcher on the counter and joined her at the kitchen table.

Mrs. Campbell's confused expression quickly melted into a smile. "Oh. You mean your father and me."

Miranda nodded. "How'd it go?" She was trying to act casual, but her eyes remained fixed on her mother's face.

"Well . . ." Her mother paused to sip her coffee. "We actually had a very nice evening. I'd been nervous about it, of course. After all, we hadn't spent any time together since he moved out of the house. But we both wanted to be there for you, and since we were both sitting in the audience it seemed silly for us to ignore each other. . . .

"Anyway, after the play, we went out for a cup of coffee."

"And?"

Her mother shrugged. "We had a good talk. For the first time in as long as I can remember, we were able to discuss things without arguing. We both let down our guards a little and tried really *listening* to what the other person was saying. . . ."

Mrs. Campbell set her coffee cup down hard. "Oh, Miranda, I shouldn't be telling you all this. It's not fair to you."

"It's okay, Mom. I'm glad you feel you can be

honest with me." Miranda reached over and gave her mother's hand a squeeze. "And I'm glad you and Dad are starting to talk."

Her mother cast her a grateful smile. Then she glanced at the clock above the stove. "It's getting late, honey. I know you had an exciting weekend, but today *is* a school day, and you're already late."

Her tone was firm, but there was a twinkle in her eyes. "Besides, aren't you anxious to get to school and hear all about how much your friends enjoyed your performance?"

Miranda laughed. "A star is born!" she joked in a melodramatic voice. And then gathering up the folds of her long red velvet gown, she headed for her room.

CHAPTER
4

As Miranda rode her bicycle to school, she was still reeling from the events of the past twenty-four hours. She struggled to get a grip on what up until very recently would have been impossible even to begin to comprehend: that the boy she loved was the victim of a hateful curse, one that caused him to shapeshift into a were-wolf.

Yet in the midst of her turmoil there was a glimmer of hope, the conviction that the knowledge she had gained—no matter how painful, no matter how overwhelming—was better than the bewilderment of not knowing. Finally she could understand Garth. And even though the monumental odds against them were now clear to her, she believed that knowing who he was, knowing *what* he was, was the first step toward making their love blossom. There would be no more confusion, no more hurt feelings . . . no more agonizing over questions that seemed to have no answers.

Something else nagged at her, a thought tucked away at the back of her mind. *If only she could help him.* If only there were some way she could free him of his curse.

That was impossible, she knew. Still, Featherwoman's words continued to echo through her head. "A terrible trial lies ahead. . . . The forces of evil have a formidable foe. The good narnauks are also powerful. . . . When the time is right, you will know."

What did it all mean? Was there any truth behind what seemed like the meaningless ramblings of an old woman? Could it be Featherwoman sensed that, somehow, there *was* a way . . . ?

Suddenly Miranda shook her head hard. For now, she would simply have to trust Garth. Be there for him. Most of all, love him, just as he was.

As she rounded a bend in the road, something suddenly caught Miranda's eye. Through the mist she could see the head of an animal. A wolf, baring its teeth, snarling savagely. Immediately she recognized it as the top of the two-hundred-year-old totem pole that loomed above the center of Overlook.

Its eyes, glowing red, burned into her.

She shuddered, then quickly looked away.

At the schoolyard, as she chained her bike to the rack, she found herself thinking about the "secret admirer" who, up until only a few weeks earlier, had been leaving love poems and little trinkets for her to find, often in the wicker basket of her bicycle. Her admirer had turned out to be Garth. His desire for secrecy, his need to hide his admiration for her, had been just one more sign of his belief that their love could never be—that she, or anyone else for that matter, could never accept him for what he was.

It could have ended tragically: a great love unfulfilled, two broken hearts, two kindred spirits letting something wondrous slip away. Yet in the end, they had come together, their love so strong that nothing could keep them apart.

As Miranda hurried through the building, the corridors of Overlook High School were empty. Her footsteps echoed through the hollow halls. Yet through the open classroom doors, she could hear voices: teachers lecturing, students answering questions.

"I know *I'm* going," she suddenly heard someone say loudly as she neared her locker. "I'm *very* curious."

Glancing up, Miranda saw two girls she recognized as sophomores strolling through the corridor. One of them was carrying a pink hall pass.

"Me, too," the other girl said. "I've never been to a town meeting before. It sounds exciting, don't you think?"

"Are you kidding?" the first one replied. "I

heard the police are going to be there!"

Miranda's own curiosity was piqued as she turned the combination on her locker.

A town meeting? In Overlook?

Their mention of the police had caused Miranda's stomach to churn. Even without having yet had a chance to find out the details, she felt sure that it had something to do with the two recent attacks.

The bell rang, and almost instantly the corridors buzzed with activity. Students swarmed from the classrooms, talking and laughing and hurrying off to their lockers or their next classes.

Suddenly she felt a tap on her shoulder.

She whirled around, her math textbook in hand. "Elinor! Just the person I wanted to see!"

Elinor Clay's forehead was furrowed with concern. "Miranda, we have to talk." Her hazel eyes looked earnest, and she smoothed back her short blunt-cut brown hair in a nervous gesture. "What happened last night?"

This was the moment Miranda had been dreading. Of course Elinor wanted an explanation. She had been there, after all. She had seen the savage wolf come running out from the shadows as the two girls were walking back to her house after the play. The beast had headed directly toward Elinor, its teeth bared, its powerful body braced for attack.

Elinor had felt the terror, had understood, for a

few excruciating seconds, that there was no hope. And then she'd witnessed the incredible moment that had passed between Miranda and the wolf.

And now she wanted an explanation for something that was nearly impossible to understand.

Miranda knew she *couldn't* tell Elinor the truth.

She turned away, pretending to be looking for a book in her locker. "I wanted to thank you for calling my mother and telling her I was staying at your house. Otherwise I would have been in big trouble." She tried to sound casual.

"I wasn't sure I was doing the right thing. I—I didn't know if I should call the police . . . or *what.*"

"You did the right thing," Miranda assured her. "And I really appreciate it."

"Miranda, I—"

"Elinor, have you heard anything about a town meeting?" she said, quickly trying to change the subject. "I heard some girls talking about it."

"Yes. It's Wednesday night at eight, at the Playhouse."

"Are you planning to go?"

"I can't. I'm baby-sitting." Elinor smoothed her hair back once again, this time in a gesture of impatience. "Miranda, we have to tell someone about what happened. We *can't* just—"

Miranda slammed her locker shut. "I'd better get moving. I've already missed my first few classes, and I don't want to be late—"

"Miranda!" Elinor grabbed her arm. "Talk to

me! What's going on? Where did you go last
night? Please, trust me. I want to know!"

Miranda looked into her eyes and saw the
pleading look there. She saw the hurt, the bewilderment, the concern. . . .

*Already my knowledge of Garth's secret is keeping
me apart . . . even from the people I feel closest to,*
Miranda thought, her heart constricting.

She looked away. "I have to go."

"Miranda!"

As she hurried away, Miranda resisted the
urge to glance over her shoulder. She knew
what she would see. Elinor standing in front of
her locker, watching the girl she thought was
her friend walking away from her.

Miranda's stomach knotted as she headed
into the crowd. She knew what she was doing to
Elinor. She could feel Elinor's frustration and
confusion as if it were her own.

Yet what caused her even more agony was
knowing that this was only the beginning.

This is what it means to live with Garth's secret,
she thought. *This is part of the torment. Part of the
horror. Part of the burden of the curse.*

Yet, as she rounded the corner, Miranda
forced her mouth into a smile, doing her best to
act as if this were just another day at school.

Her uncomfortable feelings about having to
keep her secret from Elinor, whom she'd only
recently gotten to know but who had already

proven herself a good and sincere friend, were just beginning to fade. And then, outside the classroom of her fourth-period class, she saw Selina Lamont waiting for her.

Although Selina was petite—just under five feet two—she tended to stand out in a crowd. It was partly because she was pretty, with stylishly short dark-brown hair and arresting green eyes, but it was mostly because of her penchant for wearing bright colors. Today she was decked out in a bright red, orange, and yellow minidress with orange tights. Usually the effect of Selina's wild color choices was lighthearted and fun, but lately it had been coming off as aggressive . . . almost threatening.

"Hello, Miranda," Selina said coldly.

"Hi, Selina." Miranda returned the greeting with as much enthusiasm as she could muster. The truth was that she was always on guard around Selina. These days, at least.

The two girls had been friends almost as long as she could remember—since the first grade, when they'd banded together with Corinne Davis to form friendships so solid they had lasted more than a decade. Yet recently things had changed. The trouble had begun when Miranda first learned she'd been chosen to audition for the Pacific Players' production of *Saint Joan*—and that Corinne had also been one of the five girls from Overlook High given the same honor.

She and Corinne had been in competition with each other for as long as Miranda could remember. Yet it had always been in fun. When the auditions came up, Corinne suddenly pitted herself against Miranda, setting herself up as her archrival. "I really want this part," she had told Miranda, her voice icy, "and I intend to get it."

Selina had immediately taken Corinne's side, suggesting that Miranda drop out altogether. "You know, spare yourself the humiliation of losing," Selina had said, only half teasing.

Now Corinne was home, confined to her bed, slowly recovering from both the physical and the emotional trauma of a brutal attack in the woods surrounding Overlook, not far from Cedar Crest. She was still in a state of delirium, unable to remember what had happened. Only Miranda knew the true story—Miranda . . . and Garth.

Despite Miranda's despair over Corinne's attack, Selina remained confrontational . . . accusatory, even. Just last night, after the play, Selina had condemned Miranda for taking the role, saying that it had rightfully belonged to Corinne. And so today, Miranda was wary.

Selina clasped her books tightly against her chest. "I never got the chance to tell you what I thought of the play."

"No, you didn't." Miranda's tone was guarded.

Selina hesitated a moment. "The Pacific Players

were terrific. They put on a great performance."

"I'm glad you liked it."

A heavy silence followed. The question of who really deserved the lead role continued to hover between them. The last thing she expected was for Selina to let down her icy facade.

And so she was astonished when Selina said, "You were wonderful, Miranda."

For a moment Miranda just stared at her. Selina's green eyes were clouded, her face drawn.

"Oh, Selina! I feel just as terrible as you do! Every time I think of what Corinne must have gone through, what she's going through now . . ." Without stopping to think, Miranda threw her arms around her friend.

At first Selina was stiff, but then she collapsed against her, dissolving into sobs.

"It's so awful!" Selina cried. "Why did this have to happen, Miranda? Why Corinne?"

"There's no way to make any sense out of any of it." Miranda clung to her hard, overwhelmed by the sorrow, the fear . . . the regret.

Still, it was a relief to let herself go, to share the pain with someone who, like her, loved Corinne Davis like a sister. "I'm sure she'll come through this," said Miranda. "She has to. The doctors say that all she needs is a little time. Besides, don't forget that she's a real fighter."

"You're right, Miranda. I know. She'll be

fine," Selina said, sounding as if she were trying to convince herself that it was true.

"I've been planning to visit her," said Miranda. "I know her mother said she doesn't seem aware that anyone else is in the room, but maybe she'd be able to feel deep down that there are people around who really care about her."

When she and Selina finally let go of each other, Miranda stood opposite her friend, studying her, glad that the old Selina was back.

And then Bobby McCann and Amy Patterson appeared. They came down the hall together, draped around each other as if each were incapable of standing up without leaning on the other for support.

Bobby's expression changed when he caught sight of Miranda. He stood up straighter, loosening his hold on Amy.

"Hi, Miranda," he greeted her stiffly after nodding hello to Selina.

Miranda studied her old boyfriend, remembering how attracted she had once been to him. He was good-looking—tall and lean, every inch the basketball star he'd become since sprouting up past six feet and joining the school's varsity team. Today, his dark brown hair was in need of combing, as it so often was. He kept brushing it out of his hazel eyes.

Yes, Bobby McCann was considered one of the

most desirable guys at school. But standing face to face with him this morning, Miranda felt nothing.

Even more surprising to her was the fact that she didn't feel even the slightest pang of jealousy. Even though Bobby had been *her* boyfriend just a few weeks before, she didn't blame Amy. Miranda understood now that the other girl's flirting and fawning over Bobby hadn't been the real cause of their break-up; it had been a long time coming. Bobby had wanted more than she was ready to give to him. A constant tension had lingered between them, rarely acknowledged but always present. Now, seeing Bobby and Amy together, Miranda understood that he was finally getting what he wanted.

"How's it going?" Bobby asked, trying to sound casual.

"Great," she replied.

"You two looked pretty chummy," Amy said, casting Selina a cold look as she flipped her long blond hair over one shoulder. Miranda watched as Selina's expression instantly changed to one of guilt.

"Miranda and I were just talking about the play."

"Oh, yes. The play." Amy turned her attention to Miranda. She looked her up and down, her eyes burning into Miranda with such intensity that she grew uneasy.

"I'll see ya, I'm late for class," Selina said hurriedly and darted down the hall. Miranda looked after her, disappointed.

"Great job, Miranda," Bobby said. "That was some performance." He cast Amy a furtive glance before adding, "I knew you were good, but I had no idea."

"Thanks, Bobby." She smiled at him warmly, truly appreciative of his praise.

"The whole cast did an awesome job," he added, as if he wanted to prolong the conversation. Miranda could feel Amy getting annoyed.

"All I ask is that this Friday night's performance go as well," she said.

"I hope this theater thing doesn't keep you busy all weekend," said Bobby. "I'm throwing a little party Saturday night."

Amy's mouth twisted into a pout as she turned to Bobby and said, as if Miranda weren't standing right there, "I thought we decided to keep it small."

"Miranda's always welcome at my house," he said firmly, looking at Miranda.

"If it's a problem," said Miranda, "I don't have to—"

"No. I insist. And bring your friend. You know, the guy you brought to the Homecoming Dance."

Suddenly the expression on Amy's face changed. "Yes, Miranda, bring him along," she cooed. "I think we'd all love the chance to get to know your new heartthrob better."

CHAPTER
5

The auditorium of the Overlook Playhouse was packed, Miranda observed as she and her mother made their way inside just before eight on Wednesday evening. In addition to nearly filling the rows of metal folding chairs, people stood lined up against the sides of the room or sat on the windowsills.

She recognized quite a few of the people who'd come out for this town meeting. The minister from the First Presbyterian Church, Reverend Parker, was there, as was the high school principal, Ms. Kelly. Many students from her school were there, most of them with their parents. She waved to Laura Ames and Dawn Curley, two girls from her theater class.

Yet the group did not include only residents of Overlook, she surmised from the snippets of conversation she overheard. There were also people from several neighboring towns.

Scanning the crowd, what struck her most was how many of the faces she saw looked angry.

"Look at all these people!" she said to her mother as the two of them settled into seats toward the back. "They all look like they're ready to burn down the building."

"Everyone's frightened," her mother replied. "Overlook is the kind of place where people aren't accustomed to even the smallest crime. And now two such bizarre events, so close together—"

"I know," Miranda said, trying to keep her voice even. "It's really horrible."

Miranda started as Margaret Donahue stuck her face between her and her mother. She'd been sitting behind them—and, Miranda now realized, listening to every word they'd said.

"It's inexcusable," Margaret Donahue interjected, her voice a loud hiss. While she seemed to be talking to Miranda and her mother, she spoke loudly enough to be heard by people all around, even over the din of the crowded auditorium.

"Hello, Mrs. Donahue," Miranda said evenly, her previous encounter with the woman still fresh in her mind. It had been a few weeks earlier, back at the beginning of October.

Miranda had been at the Overlook Grocery after school, and had run into Mrs. Donahue and her friend, Virginia Swensen—Andy's mother—at the back of the store.

When Featherwoman came in, the two women had been extremely rude to her, making ignorant cracks about "Indians," as they called the Native Americans that still populated the area.

"She probably needs some herbs for one of her magic potions," Mrs. Swensen had said.

"Careful, Virginia," Margaret Donahue returned. "You don't want to get scalped."

When Miranda had protested at their behavior, the two women had seemed shocked, and then Mrs. Donahue whispered something to her friend behind her hand.

Looking back on that day, Miranda suddenly remembered how Featherwoman had fixed her gaze upon Virginia Swensen as she'd sailed past her in the small store. The old Native American woman's jet-black eyes had been so piercing, so cold, that they'd made Miranda shudder. Now, Mrs. Swensen's son, Andy, was dead, the first victim of what the local paper had called the "mysterious night stalker."

That fatal attack, along with the attack on Corinne Davis twenty-nine days later, was the reason this meeting had been called. Just thinking about what was to come made Miranda's stomach tighten.

"Something must be done," Mrs. Donahue went on. "Two such horrible attacks. We've got one child in shock, the other . . . well, I don't have to tell you what Virginia and her husband, Walter, have been going through. With that dear son of theirs gone, I don't know how the two of them are going to manage to . . . why, here they come now!"

Miranda, relieved by the interruption, craned her neck so she could see the back of the auditorium. The Swensens had just arrived, their arms closely intertwined as if each were leaning on the other for support. The crowd parted, the people standing nearby growing silent as they let the bereaved couple pass.

"Poor Virginia!" Mrs. Donahue exclaimed, her voice lowered to a hoarse whisper. "She looks as if she's aged twenty years." She stood up and began pushing her way past the others seated in her row.

Miranda watched as the two women met up in the aisle, hugging each other as everyone else looked on.

"How very sad," Mrs. Campbell sighed. "I can't imagine what it must feel like to lose a child. What kind of boy was Andy?"

Miranda hesitated. She didn't want to speak ill of the dead, but the truth was that Andy Swensen had been anything but nice. In fact, he had a reputation around school for being a bully.

In the weeks prior to his death, he had singled Miranda out, making her life difficult and embarrassing her every chance he got. The night of his attack was no exception. At the

Homecoming Dance, he'd tried to goad her into dancing with him, and when she refused he grabbed hold of her dress, tearing it.

Instead of showing remorse, he'd simply laughed, saying something about how it was her fault for being so stuck-up.

Those were the last words he'd ever said to her. A few hours later, he was dead.

"Let's get started!" A confident voice, amplified by a sound system, suddenly cut through the noisy room. Turning to face the stage, where only days before she had been Saint Joan, Miranda saw that the mayor of Overlook, Tad Blackwell, was standing before the crowd, clutching a microphone. His forehead was creased with concern, and he kept running his fingers through his head of thick silvery-white hair. "We have a lot to discuss tonight, so let's get right down to business."

"We've got a killer on our hands!" a man sitting in front called out. "And we've got to stop him. That's tonight's business!"

"What are the police doing to find this maniac?" a woman yelled from the back of the room. "Why aren't our tax dollars being used to catch the killer?"

Mayor Blackwell held out his hands. "Please, folks. I know temperatures are running high tonight. We're all upset about the two recent attacks. I'm sure everybody in this room has some-

thing to say about what's being done about it—
or what's *not* being done about it.

"But I'd like you to hold your questions until
later. First we're going to hear from Officer Vale,
the police officer in charge of the investigation.
She'll be able to answer your questions about
what's been happening, and what the police
know about the individual responsible for the attacks, based on the evidence they have so far.

"We'll open the floor for questions or com-
ments after she's said her piece. Officer Vale,
without further delay, I'm going to hand the
mike over to you."

Miranda leaned forward, growing tense as a
slender woman dressed in uniform emerged
from the crowd. Miranda had talked with
Officer Vale twice before—the night she'd come
across Andy's body in the forest, and right after
Corinne's attack. The policewoman had been
extremely warm and understanding, and had
put Miranda right at ease.

Of course, back then, Miranda had known
nothing about the identity of the attacker, so she'd
had nothing to hide. But things had changed.
Now she was concealing a terrible secret.

"Thank you for giving me this opportunity to
address you regarding the recent attacks here in
Overlook," Officer Vale began. "I'd like you all
to know that the police are giving this case our
utmost attention, and that—"

"When are you going to catch the maniac?" the same woman who'd called out before yelled from the back of the room.

"Can you guarantee our safety?" a girl that Miranda recognized as a junior from her school demanded. "We're afraid to go out at night!"

The police officer held up her hand. "The police department has issued several recommendations. The first is that everyone avoid going out at night, since both attacks occurred after dark. The second is that anyone who does go out should make a point of not doing so alone. Please, travel in groups. Keep in mind that the individuals who were attacked were alone.

"The third recommendation is that the forests be avoided. Once again, the location of both attacks was in the wilds surrounding Overlook. They're dark, they're isolated, and in the woods it's virtually impossible to dust for fingerprints or find other clues. In other words, they're prime territory for a murderer. Again, don't go into the forests.

"The police force has put extra officers on special duty. We'll be following this same procedure until the perpetrator is caught. . . ."

Miranda looked around at the crowd. Naturally she wanted to side with them, to share their concerns. And she did feel for Andy and Corinne, at least as much as the others in the room.

But her first loyalty was to Garth. She was so afraid for him, afraid that sooner or later somebody would put the pieces together and the truth would come out. Yet he was innocent. It was the power that drove him, the evil force that made him do what he'd done.

"There's one more thing I want to say," Officer Vale went on. "If you or your friends have any bit of information at all, even something that you think is insignificant, please report it to the police. If you hear something, if you suspect something, I can't urge you strongly enough . . ."

Suddenly Amy Patterson stood up. Her eyes were bright, her jaw set firmly. Miranda braced herself.

"Officer Vale," she said, her voice confident and self-possessed, "I don't know if you're aware of it, but there've been some rumors circulating around town. I think the police would be wise to listen to what people have been saying—"

"I'm sorry," Officer Vale interrupted. "I guess I didn't make myself clear. The police department is interested in hearing what everyone has to say, but this is not the proper forum. If you'll come by the station or wait until after this meeting's been adjourned—"

"There's a new guy who's been hanging around lately," Amy went on, ignoring the police officer's words. "Nobody knows anything about him. Well, *almost* nobody."

She paused to look around the room. Involuntarily Miranda averted her eyes.

"Anyway, a lot of people think it's more than a coincidence that the attacks occurred right after this guy showed up."

The police officer's lips were drawn into a straight line. "As I said before, this is not the time or place to get into rumors—"

"I think somebody needs to investigate him." Amy's eyes had a cruel glint. "Maybe the police think they're doing enough, but *we* don't."

A murmur rose up from the crowd. Within seconds someone else had stood up.

"I second the motion! We've got to find out more about this Garth Gautier!"

A chill ran down Miranda's spine, not only because of what she'd heard, but because Selina Lamont had said it.

Just as the shock registered, another voice broke through the crowd. A man who'd appeared at the side door stepped forward, his manner calm yet authoritative.

"Excuse me, but I think I have something worthwhile to add." He spoke in a controlled voice. Immediately the crowd quieted down.

Miranda's heart flip-flopped. It was her father. She'd had no idea he was coming tonight. As she watched the angry mob quiet down to listen, Miranda felt incredibly proud of him.

"I believe many of you know me. My name is Bryan Campbell. I'm a veterinarian, and I have an office over in Norton. Before anybody starts pointing the finger, I think there's something the people who live in this area ought to know." Gesturing toward the police officer, he added, "I think you know where I intend to go with this."

Officer Vale nodded. "Go ahead, Dr. Campbell."

"I've seen the victims of the two attacks. The police called me in as a consultant. They had their suspicions about the nature of the wounds inflicted—"

"What's your point, Dr. Campbell?" an older man called out from the audience.

Miranda's father took a deep breath. "My point is that there's a very good chance the perpetrator wasn't a man at all. Given the wounds that were inflicted on both victims, my professional opinion is that it was an animal."

"No way! That's just some cockamamie idea the local reporters came up with to sell newspapers," the same person insisted, dismissively waving his hand in the air.

"I have to disagree." Dr. Campbell cleared his throat. "I examined both Andy Swensen and Corinne Davis. Their wounds were similar enough to conclude they were inflicted by the same individual. It's not necesary to go into the details right now, although if anyone wants to talk to me after the meeting, I'd be happy to share whatever information the police department has authorized me to speak about. Let it suffice to say again that given the nature of the wounds, their size, and their placement, my professional opinion is that they were the result of an animal attack."

"What kind of animal?" someone called out. "A bear? A coyote? A wild dog?"

"No," Dr. Campbell replied. "I'd say it was a wolf. A wolf much larger than any that's ever been spotted around these parts, but a wolf nonetheless."

A man stood up in the back of the room, waving his fist angrily in the air. "How do we know you're not just telling us what the police want us to hear?"

"I think it's a man," someone else cried. "I've lived here in the Pacific Northwest fifty-three years, and I've never heard of a wolf attacking a person!"

"And what if it is an animal?" a third voice called out. "What's being done to catch it—and kill it?"

Officer Vale took the microphone from Dr. Campbell. "Please, let's address the questions one at a time. There's time for everyone to speak. But I think the most important thing to keep in mind is that the best we can do until we've found out all the answers is to keep ourselves safe."

By the time the meeting ended, Miranda's head was spinning. The auditorium had begun to feel claustrophic, as if there wasn't enough air. She longed to be outdoors, inhaling the cold freshness of the night.

"I'll meet you at home later," she told her mother, hastily pulling on her jacket. "I have to get out for a while."

"Miranda!" Mrs. Campbell exclaimed. "You heard what Officer Vale said. It's not safe to—"

But Miranda was already pushing her way through the crowd that was slowly filing out of the auditorium.

Needing to be outdoors was only part of the reason for her sudden flight. Even more, she had to see Garth.

I have to find him, she thought as she wove desperately through the mass of people. *I have to warn him.*

She was near the theater's back door when she heard someone call her name.

"Miranda? Wait!"

Glancing up, she saw Laura Ames and Dawn Curley heading her way.

"Garth Gautier is your boyfriend, isn't he?" Laura asked, breathless as she caught up with her.

Miranda nodded.

"That's what we thought," said Dawn. "We saw you with him at the Homecoming Dance."

"We just want you to know that not everybody at school thinks he's linked to the attacks," Laura said, looking apologetic. "It's just not fair, the way people like Amy and Selina are trying to pin this on him."

Dawn nodded. "Don't listen to them, Miranda. Hardly anybody else is taking them seriously."

"Thank you." Miranda could feel her eyes growing moist. "You don't know how much this means to me."

She turned away, rushing out into the night.

"Garth! Garth, are you here?"

Miranda stepped into Cedar Crest through the front door, which had seemed to beckon her inside. She was desperate to see him, to tell him what had happened at the town meeting. Even more, she longed to have him quell her growing fears.

"Miranda!" He emerged from the shadows, pausing in the entryway of the front parlor.

"Oh, Garth. I'm so glad I found you."

She reached up and embraced him. His strong arms encircled her, pulling her close against him. She could feel his heart beating steadily, a marked contrast to her own, pounding at a wild pace. Yet it was already growing calmer. Just being near him comforted her. His mere presence was capable of banishing most of the demons that taunted her, instilling her with uncertainties that tore at her heart.

Lovingly he smoothed her hair with his large, powerful hands. "What's wrong?"

"I just came from the town meeting—"

"Come. Sit down." Taking her by the hand, Garth led Miranda into the front parlor.

The walls of the room were covered in dark, elegant wallpaper, creating a welcoming atmosphere, as if in here she could be safe. A fire burned brightly in the marble fireplace, its flames providing the only illumination, making it difficult for her to see his face.

There was little furniture in the room: only a couch, covered in gold brocade, its mahogany legs carved into elaborate scrolls. On the highly polished wooden floor in front of the fireplace lay a richly colored Oriental rug.

The two of them sat down on the gold couch, Miranda perching anxiously on the edge. She could see his face now. A wave of warmth rushed over her as she saw the concern in his blue eyes, the tension in his mouth and forehead as he waited to hear what was troubling her.

"All right," he said, his voice soothing. "Tell me everything."

"Mayor Blackwell called the meeting to alert everyone in the area to what's been happening." She took a deep breath. "To talk about the attacks."

"Go on."

"It was packed, Garth. People came from all

over. Officer Vale spoke. You remember her, don't you?"

Garth nodded. "At the police station. The night you came across Andy's body in the woods."

"Right. She told the group the police had added extra forces to patrol the area. Still, she recommended that people stay in at night—and if they do go out, that they not travel alone. She also warned everyone about going into the forest."

"But none of this is what has you so upset, is it?"

"No." Miranda hesitated before going on, afraid of how what she was about to say might affect him. "Amy Patterson stood up and publicly accused you of being the person responsible for the attacks."

She searched his face, anxious about his reaction. Yet he remained impassive. "What was even worse was that Selina agreed with her."

"I see. How did the others respond?"

"Officer Vale insisted it wasn't the time and place to make accusations. That ended that, at least for the moment." Miranda thought back for a moment, remembering what Dawn and Laura had said. "A couple of girls I know from school made a point of telling me they thought what Amy and Selina were saying was terrible. They also told me hardly anyone else thinks you're involved. It made me feel better to know that most people aren't in such a hurry to point the finger."

Garth simply nodded.

"But it was my father who was the most helpful."

"Your father!"

She nodded. "Since he's a veterinarian, he was called in by the police as a consultant. They were investigating the possibility that the wounds on both Andy and Corinne had been inflicted by an animal, not a man. My father stood up at the meeting and told everyone what his conclusions were, that a human being couldn't possibly have been responsible. That helped quiet Amy and Selina."

"Ah, Miranda." Woefully Garth shook his head. "I wish . . . I wish—"

"Yes, Garth?"

"I wish things weren't so complicated. I wish there were no one in the world but us, nothing for you and me to think about but our love." He threw back his head, his face an expression of despair. "How I long to protect you from all this!"

Miranda was suddenly filled with fear. "Oh, Garth. What's going to happen to us?"

"Miranda, my love." Leaning forward, he took her in his arms. Gently he pressed her face against his chest. "It breaks my heart to think the love I feel for you could cause you even the slightest worry."

"Sometimes I get so afraid."

"Afraid of what people like Amy and Selina might do?"

Miranda reached up and stroked his cheek

with her hand. "Afraid that our love won't be strong enough to withstand the trials that still lie before us."

"Don't ever be afraid of that." Garth's lips were soft and warm against her forehead. "There's never been a love as strong as ours. Don't you feel it?"

Pulling back slightly, Miranda looked up into Garth's eyes. She knew in her heart that he was right. Their love *was* special, far beyond anything she had ever felt, far beyond even the great loves she had read about in books.

Yet the odds against them seemed so insurmountable. And the people of Overlook, people like Amy and Selina, who seemed determined to destroy them, were only the beginning.

Even more powerful was the evil force that held Garth in its merciless grip. Miranda knew the evil would fight their love—so strong, so pure, so unselfish—the minute it proved to be an obstacle.

In the end, the malevolent evil power was their most formidable foe—an enemy she knew instinctively was potent enough to destroy anything in its path.

Arriving home late that night, Miranda was careful not to make any noise. She pulled off her shoes before creeping across the front hallway of her house, slowly making her way through the darkness.

Suddenly she saw that the living room was illuminated by lamplight.

"Mom?" Miranda stepped across the hallway. She found her mother curled up on the couch, in a nightgown and a bathrobe. The television was on, the sound of a late-night movie turned down so low it was barely audible.

Mrs. Campbell blinked. "What time is it?"

"It's after midnight."

Miranda's mother glanced at her wristwatch. "It's almost two o'clock!" Turning to Miranda, she said in a gentle voice, "Miranda, it's very late."

Gingerly Miranda lowered herself onto the chair opposite her. "I know, Mom. And I realize it's a school night."

"Yes, it is. But it's not only that." Mrs. Campbell pulled her robe more tightly around her. "You were with Garth, weren't you?"

"Yes."

"I thought so." She hesitated. "Miranda, I'm not about to tell you how to live your life. You are a young woman, after all, not a little girl. . . ."

"I know what I'm doing," Miranda assured her.

"I've known for some time how important Garth is to you."

Miranda nodded. "We're in love."

"I hope everything works out for you." Mrs. Campbell thought for a few seconds before saying, "I hope, though, that staying out late like this doesn't become a pattern. I was worried."

"I'm getting all my schoolwork done," Miranda insisted.

"I know how responsible you are. Your father and I have always trusted you. And, well, maybe I'm guilty of being so wrapped up in what's been going on with my own life that I haven't been paying enough attention to you lately. But ever since the town meeting, I haven't been able to stop thinking about how dangerous it is for you to be out alone."

"I know this area, Mom. I've lived here my whole life. I can take care of myself."

"Andy and Corinne thought that, too."

Miranda lowered her eyes. She wanted to tell her mother she was perfectly safe, to allay the fears she could see were making it impossible for Mrs. Campbell to sleep.

Yet she couldn't. Once again, she had to keep silent. The truth about Garth had to remain a secret—even to her mother.

"I'll be careful, Mom. I promise."

"Could you do me a favor?"

"Anything."

"Ask Garth to stay with you whenever you're out at night. I'll feel much better, knowing he's there to protect you."

"He'll keep me safe," Miranda assured her, reaching over and squeezing her mother's hand. "I can promise you that Garth would never let anything bad happen to me."

CHAPTER
6

Thursday morning, as Miranda passed through the halls of Overlook High on her way to Mr. Wexler's first-period English class, her bad feeling about the town meeting still lingered. The crowd's anger had frightened her. Even more, she was upset by Amy's and Selina's determination to turn the town against Garth, trying to rally the others' support based on nothing more than the fact that he was an outsider.

Glancing at her watch, she realized it would be only seconds before the bell rang. Hurrying, she turned a corner. Suddenly she found herself up against a barricade. Two boys were planted directly in her path. The taller one, lanky and blond, stood with his arms folded across his chest. The other, with dark curly hair and a wiry build, leaned against the wall, his outstretched arm blocking her way. Both were smirking.

"Excuse me," Miranda said to Dave Falco and Mark O'Neill.

"'Excuse me,'" Dave echoed in a high-pitched voice.

It was the same way their friend Andy Swensen had mocked her.

One of the many times Andy had singled her out as the target for his bullying came rushing back to her, replaying in her mind like a scene from a movie. It had been in October, just a few weeks earlier, right after an episode in English class in which Andy had gotten in trouble—and had blamed the entire incident on Miranda. The following morning, he had banded together with Mark and Dave, coming up behind her while she was at her locker. One hard shove and she dropped all her schoolbooks, sending papers and texts flying across the floor.

"Oops," he'd said in a jeering tone. "Guess I'm getting clumsy in my old age."

Determined not to rise to the bait, Miranda had simply crouched down and set about retrieving her books and papers. Yet he'd persisted.

"That was some stunt you pulled with Wexler the other day," Andy had complained. "He's still on my case."

She'd glanced up at him. "I didn't mean to get you in trouble."

"'I didn't mean to get you in trouble,'" Andy

mimicked her in a high-pitched voice, much to the amusement of his two friends. Both of them burst into loud, forced laughter, meanwhile slapping him on the back.

Now Dave and Mark were doing the same thing. Singling her out, confronting her in the hall, even mimicking her, as if they'd learned all the lessons Andy had to teach. Standing face to face with them, she felt as if history were repeating itself. Her heart was pumping furiously. Yet she strove to maintain a calm exterior.

"Maybe you don't care if you're late for English," she said, her voice controlled, "but I—"

"Hey, Miranda." Mark leaned over so that his face was close to hers. A few strands of blond hair fell into his eyes. "I heard things got pretty heated at that meeting last night."

"Yeah," said Dave. "Sounds like that boyfriend of yours is in pretty deep."

Rage rose up inside Miranda. "Don't you have anything better to do than stand around gossiping?"

Snickering, Dave glanced over at Mark. "As a matter of fact, we do."

"Yeah, that's right," Mark seconded, his eyes narrowing. "Dave and me, we got big plans."

Miranda froze. "What do you mean?" Anxiously she looked from one to the other. She could tell from the expressions on their faces that whatever their "big plans" were, they added up to trouble.

Instead of answering, the two of them simply laughed. The hollowness of the sound continued ringing through Miranda's ears as she pushed her way past them and hurried away.

Sitting in English class, Miranda was unable to concentrate on Mr. Wexler's lecture on Shakespeare's tragedies. She was too busy thinking about the ugly scene in the hallway. Dave and Mark were sitting in the back of the room, a few rows behind her, and she could feel their eyes burning into her.

Staring out the window, Mr. Wexler's voice droning in the background, Miranda let her mind drift. Her encounter with Dave Falco and Mark O'Neill had brought to a head all the feelings she'd been struggling so hard to avoid. But now she was unable to stop herself from confronting them head-on.

She loved Garth. Her feelings for him were deeper than any she had ever known. When she was with him, time stopped. Nothing else existed besides him. When she was away from him, she could still feel his presence, a pocket of warmth she carried wherever she went.

She never questioned that love. The *cost* of loving him was what troubled her. Her heart ached constantly, torn by ambivalence as she tried to find a way to fit the man she loved into the rest of her life. She agonized over the worry she was causing her mother; her estrangement from Elinor, who sensed her distance yet couldn't be permitted to know the truth; the anger of some of the students at Overlook High and people in town. She, like Garth, was being cast into the role of outsider.

Yet even her alienation from everyone she cared about paled beside the turmoil raging inside. She knew what Garth was. She understood the magnitude of what she was taking on by loving him. She was already seeing the choices she had to make in order to be with him. And deep inside, she wondered if her love was really strong enough. She wondered if *she* was strong enough.

She needed to confide in someone. She desperately needed a friend. Up until now, she'd confided in her diary only, pouring out her heart on the blank pages of a book, knowing there would be no judgments, no recriminations.

Yet that wasn't enough—not now. She longed for a compassionate ear, a caring soul. Someone to sympathize. To understand. Above all, simply to listen.

Sitting at her desk, Miranda thought about the people who'd been important to her. Her oldest friends came to mind first. Yet Corinne was unreachable, a victim of the curse that haunted Garth. Selina was similarly unavailable. The fact that she was running hot and then cold made it that much more painful.

Then there was Elinor. She and Miranda had only recently become friends. And she valued that friendship. It had come at a time when she most needed support, entering her life like an unexpected gift. Now a chasm separated them. The secret she was required to keep made the closeness they had once shared an impossibility.

And Bobby, of course, was lost to her. Once he'd been her closest friend. They had shared thoughts and dreams and experiences, holding back nothing from each other. While they had begun to think of each other romantically back in the ninth grade, they had been friends since childhood. Now even he was gone. It was not the romance she missed; it was his friendship. She couldn't help but resent the fact that it had been taken away from her.

She could talk to her mother. Of everyone, she was the most understanding, the most accepting, the most eager to help. Yet Miranda's first instinct was to protect her from the pain that she, her daughter, was experiencing. Knowing Mrs. Campbell had her own problems made Miranda want to alleviate her difficulties, not add to them.

As hard as it was to face, Miranda was alone to struggle with her burden. There was no one to help. She had to reach deep inside herself, into places that in all her seventeen years had gone unexplored, and come up with the strength to carry on.

* * *

Miranda lay in Garth's arms late Thursday night, her head resting on his shoulder, the dark wavy strands of her hair strewn across his chest. Eagerly she inhaled his musky scent, while running her fingers through his thick hair. The golden strands glinted in the light from the fire burning in the marble fireplace, banishing the shadows of dusk that otherwise would have swallowed up Cedar Crest's elegant front parlor.

Usually just being with him calmed her. In his presence all her doubts and fears vanished. A sense of serenity would come over her, the heartfelt conviction that in the end everything would work out for them.

Tonight that feeling of tranquility eluded her.

Even Garth sensed it. "What is it, Miranda?" he asked, stroking her hair. "What's troubling you?"

Her first impulse was to insist that nothing was wrong. To protect him. But he knew her too well. She couldn't hide her true feelings from him any more than she could hide them from herself.

"I'm frightened."

He leaned forward, gently kissing the top of her head. "There's nothing to fear. You've said it yourself, Miranda: together, we're magic."

"We're magic to each other," she protested. "But that doesn't mean we can protect each other from what others might do to us."

She felt Garth grow tense. "Something's happened, hasn't it?"

"Yes. I wasn't sure if I should tell you."

"You have to tell me, Miranda. I should know everything."

"All right." She took a deep breath. "Two boys confronted me at school today—"

"Who?"

"Mark O'Neill and Dave Falco." Miranda paused before adding, "They were two of Andy Swensen's closest friends."

"Go on."

"They . . . they threatened me, Garth."

"Did they hurt you?" he demanded.

Miranda shook her head. "No. But they told me they had 'big plans.' When I tried to find out what they meant, they just laughed."

Involuntarily she shuddered. "I don't know what they've got up their sleeves. But I have a terrible feeling about this, Garth."

"They were probably just mouthing off," Garth insisted. "Understandably, they're angry that their friend is gone and looking for someone to blame. You were the one who found his body in the woods, so they picked you."

"There was more." She spoke slowly, choosing her words carefully. "Mark said he'd heard things got heated at the town meeting. And then Dave said something about you. That you were in pretty deep."

"I'm sure they're harmless," Garth insisted. "It sounds to me like they're nothing but a couple of kids trying to act tough."

"I hope you're right," said Miranda. "But what if you're not? What if Dave and Mark really are planning to make trouble for you?"

"I can take care of myself." Taking Miranda's hand in his, he brought it up to his lips and kissed it. "Don't forget, Miranda; I always have."

Garth stayed awake for a long time after Miranda had drifted off to sleep, the two of them stretched out in front of the dying fire, their limbs intertwined as they lay together on the thick Oriental carpet. He was thinking about how he'd deceived her.

He, too, was afraid. He knew that anger could drive people to do terrible things.

A disturbing scene ran through his mind, one that had occurred only weeks earlier. It had been the night of the last full moon, the night that he had shapeshifted into werewolf form . . . the night he had attacked Corinne Davis.

Knowing there would be a full moon that night, he had gone to great effort to try to control the beast. Deliberately he had locked himself in the basement, closing himself up in a tiny cell-like room with a thick wooden door and a single small window covered with thick metal bars.

And then he'd heard voices outside. Three in-

terlopers had snuck onto the grounds of Cedar
Crest. It was Corinne and two of her friends:
Paul, who he now knew was Corinne's boyfriend,
and Tommy, who was Selina's. He heard them
talking about shooting off firecrackers.

They wanted to scare him. Perhaps even to
hurt him. They wanted revenge. A boy at school
had been attacked . . . and those who knew him
were looking for somebody to blame. Garth was
the outsider in Overlook, and so they had chosen him. And of course, they'd been right.

Once they'd discovered they really were
brave enough to venture onto his property,
Corinne came up with the idea of breaking into
the house. She tried to talk the others into following her, but they resisted.

Corinne unwittingly opened the door of the
tiny room in which Garth had imprisoned himself. She let out the beast—and precipitated the
attack that to this day held her in a state of shock,
keeping her out of touch with herself, with those
who loved her, with the entire world around her.

Thinking about Corinne always brought him
pain. He knew he wasn't really responsible; it was
the evil curse. Yet he couldn't deny that it was *his*
powerful jaws, *his* four limbs with their animal
strength and their sharp claws, that had reduced
Miranda's friend to such a pitiable state. . . .

Suddenly he started, every muscle tensing.
He'd heard something, a sharp crackling noise.

It broke through the almost eerie silence that always enshrouded Cedar Crest as nighttime settled over land and sea.

His heart pounded and adrenaline surged through his body.

"Miranda?" he said softly, wondering if she'd heard the noise as well. But she was silent, her breaths low and even as she slept.

Moving carefully so he wouldn't wake her, he extricated himself from their embrace. Without turning any lights on, not even lighting a candle, he went over to the window. As he neared it, the crackling noise broke the silence once again.

From where he stood, close to the window but a few inches away so he couldn't be seen, Garth peered out into the night. In the dim light of the moon, he saw there were two boys outside Cedar Crest, right outside the window, the brittle leaves beneath their feet giving them away. One was tall, with light hair; the other, dark-haired.

Garth couldn't be certain, but he suspected they were the two boys Miranda had mentioned. Mark and Dave. Andy Swensen's friends.

He glanced over at her, wondering if he should wake her. She looked so relaxed, so peaceful lying on the thick red carpet, her lovely features gently illuminated by the embers.

No, he decided. He would handle this alone.

Turning back to the window, he saw that the two intruders were already moving away, heading

toward the back section of the grounds surrounding Cedar Crest. They would find little, he knew; a
greenhouse, a wooden potting shed, and on the
edge of the property, a carriage house that these
days was used for storage. Still, he was disturbed by
the boys' presence, and by the fact that he could
no longer see them—or what they were doing.

He knew he had to go out, into the night.
His familiarity with every square inch of his
property would enable him to keep hidden.

Stealthily Garth hurried through the house,
winding his way down long corridors that twisted
and turned like a maze. At the end was the
sprawling kitchen area, a complex of three large
rooms. He had frequently speculated that,
decades earlier, when Cedar Crest was still a
place that bustled with activity, they had been
used to prepare food for myriads of houseguests.
Tonight he found their unusual size an annoy-
ance, one more delay in reaching his destina-
tion.

He slipped out through a back door, finding
himself fairly close to the carriage house. Re-
maining in the shadows, Garth paused, his head
cocked to one side as he relied upon his extraor-
dinary powers of hearing to help him locate the
two trespassers.

Sure enough; he heard them talking behind
the low building that had once accommodated
up to four elegant carriages. The wooden struc-

ture was at least a hundred yards away, yet he could hear every word.

"Are you kidding? This is a great idea!" The voice belonged to Mark O'Neill, the taller, fair-haired boy.

"I don't know." Dave Falco sounded uncertain. "We could get in real trouble."

"Hey, you want to send this guy a message or not? He doesn't belong here. We don't want him. We gotta be clear about that. Got it?"

"I know, Mark, I know. But this could be dangerous."

"*Trust* me. I know what I'm doing."

"Well . . . if you're sure . . ."

Suddenly Garth inhaled sharply. His sensitive nose had picked up a familiar scent—one that set his nerves on edge. He'd heard the sound that went along with it, as well. A shushing, quickly followed by a snap.

The sound of a match being lit.

Mark's cackling laugh cut through him like a knife. "Not bad, huh? You just gotta know your way around a bottle of lighter fluid, that's all. Huh, I wish my dad could see me now. He's always complaining that I can't even light the barbecue!"

The flickering light of the flames was already apparent even though Garth was a good hundred yards from the carriage house. The fire had been set in the back corner, not far from the edge of the woods that surrounded the grounds.

Panic rose up inside him. If the flames traveled even a few feet, they would ignite the entire forest.

And then a sick feeling came over him as he was struck with another realization.

Chemicals were stored in the carriage house. Paint, kerosene, turpentine. Many of them were flammable. Some were explosive.

"Hey, check this out!" Mark's voice had grown shrill, his excitement escalating. He danced around the carriage house, lighting matches and dropping them at the edge of the building every few feet. "Am I a natural or what? This is gonna show lover boy what we think of outsiders. Especially outsiders who just happen to show up around the time a psycho starts hanging out in the woods!"

Garth didn't even feel the change coming upon him. It happened too quickly, in a fraction of a second. All of a sudden he found himself low to the ground. He sprang toward the carriage house, which was by now completely aflame. He was still enough of a human being to realize what had happened—with a speed heretofore unknown to him, he had made the transformation into a werewolf.

He waited, expecting his mind to grow clouded. But his thought processes remained unchanged.

His senses were more acute than ever. His nostrils stung from the smell of sulfur and burning wood. His ears smarted at the loud crackling of the flames leaping up the sides of the building. His eyes narrowed as the brightness of the light assaulted them.

Yet none of that deterred him. Only one thought filled his mind, still as clear as when he'd been in human form. And that was that he had to stop them.

He meant them no harm. His intention was to frighten them, to banish them from Cedar Crest before any more damage was done. To put a hasty end to this hideous assault, along with their outrageous notions about avenging their friend's death.

He came upon the shorter boy first. He was standing a few feet back from the carriage house, his eyes wide, his expression one of horror. Yet whether it was the fire that had him so agitated or the crazed behavior of his friend, still circling the building, tossing matches wildly, Garth couldn't say.

Then the boy turned, his eyes lighting on the beast that approached him. The look on his face turned to one of pure terror.

"Mark, look out!" he screamed, scrambling backward toward the forest.

"I'm doing fine," Mark shot back, not even glancing over. "Leave me alone."

"Mark! It's—" And then the wolf was upon him. Rising up on his hind legs, he flung him-

self forward, his front paws squarely hitting
Dave's shoulders. He knocked him down easily,
the boy's bulk offering little resistance to the animal's powerful muscles.

Immediately Garth backed off, crouching a
few feet away from the petrified boy. He snarled,
raising his lips so that his sharp white teeth were
bared.

By now, Dave was unable to utter a sound. He
simply lay on the ground, frozen. He had turned
white, his eyes, wild with fear, glued to the giant
werewolf. Mark was on the other side of the carriage house now, still oblivious to the beast.

"Hey, aren't you gonna help me? Not that
there's much to do. I pretty much covered this
baby. How about hitting the house next?"

Mark rounded the corner of the burning
building, his stride confident, almost arrogant.
And then he, too, froze.

"Run!" Dave suddenly yelled. "Get out of here!"

Mark took a step backward. And then he
stopped. His eyes narrowing, he reached for a
plank of wood that had fallen off the carriage
house. One end was aflame.

"Get out of here, you mangy cur!" He rushed toward Garth, clutching the torch in his right hand.

The beast stood very still, facing him, waiting. And then, when he was only a few inches
away, in one smooth, graceful movement he
jumped to the side. Mark, caught off guard,

stumbled. He sprawled across the uneven ground, falling onto the burning piece of wood.

He let out a loud, ungodly cry. Garth recoiled in horror. When the boy rolled across the ground, still wailing, Garth saw that his shirt was on fire.

"Mark!" Dave shrieked. With jerky movements he started to move toward his friend. Then, glancing at the wolf, he instead stayed where he was.

In a swift and unexpected movement, Mark, still yelling in pain, flung the torch outward. It landed at the edge of the woods, immediately setting a tall cedar afire. Within seconds the flames devoured the entire tree, then spread to a clump of low bushes nearby.

Garth watched in horror. The fire was out of control. He could smell the chemicals in the carriage house. He knew they were quickly heating up in their metal containers. Mark lay on the ground, howling, his charred shirt sticking to the burns on his stomach.

And then he became aware of the presence of another. He turned, knowing not through his five senses but through some other means that Miranda was near. She stood outside the back door, her hair still tousled, her face twisted into an expression of shock as she looked on.

"No!" she cried, the lone syllable rising up from deep inside.

The smell of the chemicals inside the carriage house was growing stronger with each passing

second. At the edge of the forest, the fire spread
with alarming speed. Swiftly it traveled across the
underbrush, passing from tree to tree, the flames
reaching up ten, fifteen, twenty feet high.

His initial urge was to protect her. To get her
away from this horrible scene . . . before it was too
late. He tried to yell, to warn her to keep away. Yet
when he opened his mouth, the only sound that
escaped was the mournful howl of a wolf.

He leapt toward her, hoping he could will her
to understand. She paid him no heed. Instead, she
came toward him, toward the burning carriage
house, toward the forest hot and bright with flame.

Her pace was slow, almost as if she were walking in her sleep. Her bare feet crossed sharp
stones and coarse gravelly spots without pain reg-
istering on her face. With glassy eyes Miranda
stared straight ahead, not even glancing to the
side as she moved toward the carriage house.
Garth wondered if she could actually see the de-
struction, the insanity before her.

And then she stopped, halfway between the
carriage house and the burning forest. Her face
was illuminated with an orange glow. The heat
from the fire, only a few feet away on either
side, was intense. Garth backed away, his bestial
instincts warning him to keep his distance.

Still, he longed to drag Miranda far from the
flames, to get both of them away from the danger. But something in her movements prevented

him from taking any action. Instead he watched, mesmerized by the ease with which she walked through the burning tunnel.

And then, raising her face toward the sky, extending her hands palms upward, she muttered that single syllable once again.

"*No!*"

She closed her eyes. For a few seconds, nothing happened. And then, slowly, a beatific smile began spreading across her face.

At first Garth was astonished. And then he heard it. He felt it, too. Large drops of cool water, falling from the sky.

Rain.

Within seconds a steady downpour began, the most furious sheeting rain he had ever seen. The air was silver, transformed by the vertical lines of water that shot down like the cascades of a waterfall.

Already the fire was being beaten down. The flames in the forest grew less enthusiastic, getting lower and lower as if they'd given up the fight. The carriage house quickly became soaked.

New smells emerged. Smoldering wood. Damp earth. And ash—wonderful, glorious ash—a sign that at last the fire had been defeated.

"Let's move!" Dave cried, jumping off the ground. Reaching down, he pulled on Mark's arm. "Come on, Mark. We gotta get out of here!"

His face twisted with pain, Mark dragged himself up off the ground. He let out a groan.

"Come on. I'll get you to a doctor. But you gotta run, man!" Dave cried.

As they were stumbling across the ground, Miranda turned to face them.

"You won't tell anyone," she said, her voice commanding.

Dave and Mark just stared at her.

"If you do," she went on, "I'll tell them what happened. I'll tell them it was all your fault!"

"Let's get outta here," Mark insisted.

Yet as they tried to run, they fell, as if their ankles were being held to the ground.

"Promise!" Miranda cried.

"Okay! Okay! We promise, we promise!" Dave's voice was pleading. "Just let us go."

"I'll hold you to your word," Miranda said firmly.

This time their struggle to run was successful. The two boys disappeared into the woods, Dave holding on to Mark's arm as he helped him cross the hostile terrain.

Garth could feel himself changing back to human form. The transformation was quick, so quick that he didn't know it was happening until he found himself standing face to face with Miranda. Behind her, great coils of black smoke rose up from the forest. Turning around, he saw that the carriage house, though badly burned, still stood. The smell of charred wood hung heavily in the air.

The damage had been great. Yet he and Miranda were both safe. And that, he knew, as he took her face gently in his hands, running his thumbs along the soft skin of her cheeks, was all that mattered.

"Miranda," Garth said once they'd gone back into the house, "how did you do it?"

"I didn't do it," she told him, gazing at him from where she sat curled up on the gold brocade couch, her dark eyes bright and her cheeks flushed with exhilaration. "The power came from somewhere else."

His initial reaction of astonishment quickly faded to acceptance. "I understand. It was rooted in something good. Something positive."

Miranda nodded. "The good narnauks. It had to have been their power."

"You felt their presence?"

"Yes. Oh, Garth, it was such a wonderful feeling! I could feel their positive energy, carrying me forward, instilling me with such miraculous abilities. . . . It was their power and our love, Garth, that enabled us to fight. That was what saved Cedar Crest . . . that was what saved us."

"Yes," he said simply.

His thoughts were far away as he stroked Miranda's hair. Yet he chose not to verbalize what disturbed him so: that if the power of goodness was intervening in Miranda's life, the power of evil was not far behind.

CHAPTER
7

Friday night, as she walked down the meandering path toward the Overlook Playhouse, instead of trying to get in character for that evening's performance of *Saint Joan*, Miranda was worrying about the reports she'd heard at school that day. Rumors about Mark O'Neill were flying. Word of his second-degree burns had traveled quickly. Already students who knew him were sending flowers or making plans to visit him at the hospital.

Yet there was still speculation about how he had gotten injured in the first place. Dave Falco was insisting the two of them had simply been trying to burn a pile of leaves, intending to make a bonfire. Even so, the fact that the accident had happened on the edge of Cedar Crest's property had some people wondering about what had actually happened.

At least Garth hasn't been accused of involvement, Miranda reminded herself, finding little comfort in that thought as she pulled open the door of the theater and stepped out of the raw November night and into the welcoming warmth of the wooden building's lobby.

She noticed her hands were trembling, but it wasn't Dave Falco who was responsible nor the cold, nor even nervousness over that evening's performance. It was knowing that tonight she'd be seeing Elinor, who was the assistant stage manager in the Pacific Players' production of *Saint Joan*.

All week, the two girls had avoided each other. The few times their paths had crossed at school, Elinor's only response had been a confused, hurt look.

So as Miranda's footsteps clicked against the lobby's black and white marble floor, she felt weighed down by her dread of the inevitable confrontation—and the fact that she had yet to come up with an explanation for the bizarre events of five nights earlier.

She spotted Elinor backstage standing with a group of other crew members. Her cheeks were flushed.

Miranda went right up to her, suddenly anxious to get it over with.

"Elinor—"

"Oh, hi, Miranda." Elinor's reserved reception didn't come as a surprise, given Miranda's evasiveness the last time they'd spoken.

"Could we go somewhere to talk?"

"Sure." Elinor tucked the script she'd been marking with a red pencil under her arm and led Miranda to a quiet corner, back where coils of thick black lighting cables were stored. "Shoot."

Miranda took a deep breath. "I just wanted to say that I'm sorry I've been acting so strange all week. I've been really upset about what happened Sunday night. I don't know how to explain it . . . and I guess I just wanted to forget it."

"Forget it? You saved my life, Miranda!" There was awe in Elinor's voice. "But—but how did you do it?"

"I didn't do anything," Miranda insisted. "The wolf probably ran off because he got frightened. Maybe your screaming scared him off."

"I guess . . . it's just that I got this strange feeling. It was almost as if . . . as if you were actually communicating with that animal, Miranda."

"But that's impossible, Elinor!"

"I know. . . . But at the time—" She shook her head. "I don't know what to think. It all happened so fast. And I was practically in shock. To be perfectly honest, I'm not sure *what* happened."

She thought for a few seconds before adding, "I think we should tell the police."

"But nothing happened!"

"It *almost* did. If that wolf hadn't gotten scared, if he hadn't turned and run away back into the

woods—" Elinor shuddered. "That might have
been the same animal that attacked Corinne and
Andy Swensen. Maybe it's rabid, Miranda. I've
never seen a wild animal act like that. Venturing
so close to civilization, coming right up to us . . . I
think we should tell somebody."

Miranda's mind raced. Her first instinct was
to protect Garth. Certainly that meant keeping
the police away. But protecting him also meant
preventing anyone else from becoming suspicious—and that included Elinor.

"All right," she agreed. "Contact the police
first thing tomorrow."

"Good. I feel better already."

"Me, too." Nervously Miranda shifted her
weight from one foot to the other. "Maybe you
and I could get together afterward. We—we
haven't had a chance to talk much lately."

Elinor smiled. "Actually, tomorrow's my birthday."

"Happy birthday!"

"Thanks. But it means my family's got the
whole day planned. Hey, maybe you'd like to
come over and have some birthday cake. I'm
warning you that there'll be a million relatives
there. But it should be fun anyway."

"I'd love to come," Miranda said, laughing.

"Great. Nine o'clock?"

"That sounds—" Miranda's smiled faded.
"Oh, Elinor. I'm so sorry. I can't make it. Bobby

McCann's giving a party, and it starts at eight."

"Oh." Elinor's cheerful expression flickered for only a moment. "Well, then, I'll save you a piece of cake."

"That'd be really nice."

Suddenly the Pacific Players' director, Tyler Fleming, appeared backstage, clapping his hands to get the attention of the cast and crew.

"Looks like it's show time," observed Elinor. "Time to say good-bye to reality and step back into the world of make-believe."

Miranda simply nodded. She wasn't about to let on that all of a sudden too much of her life seemed to be spent doing just that.

He sat at the back of the theater, alone.

He was surrounded by others, the audience captivated by the production of *Saint Joan*. Onstage a young woman was being led toward a stake, her hands tied behind her with a frayed length of rope. Pieces of wood were piled all around.

They were going to burn her. They were going to burn his Miranda.

No!

The word, one single syllable, caught in his throat. It was all he could do to keep from uttering it aloud.

Part of him knew it was only a play. But another part reacted so viscerally that it was as if he were experiencing the horror himself. He could feel the flames, their menacing heat growing stronger and stronger against his skin. He could hear their cries, see their angry faces . . . feel their hatred.

He had to get out.

Garth rushed toward the lobby, wanting only to be alone. There he sank onto a bench, burying his face in his hands. Waiting for his heart to cease its hammering, for his gasping breaths to grow calm.

He snapped his head up when he felt someone touch his shoulder lightly. His eyes locked onto a pair of dark brown eyes, peering down at him solemnly.

He'd never seen the man before. His appearance was odd enough that Garth knew he would have remembered. His skin had a weathered look; years of exposure to sun and wind had made it impossible to estimate his age. He was heavily bearded, the coarse black hairs edged with white. The bushy mass of hair sticking out from beneath the red-and-black plaid hunting cap pulled down over his head was the same wiry texture, an identical blend of colors. His nose was hooked, his yellowing teeth crooked.

Yet it was none of those features that instilled in Garth the basic fear that gripped him. It was something instinctive that warned him that danger lurked here.

Horrified, he recoiled.

"What do you want?" Garth demanded.

The man bent forward so that his face was close. "Let me help you," he hissed.

He reached out, taking hold of Garth's arm. Abruptly Garth yanked it away.

"Leave me alone!" he cried. Already he was halfway across the lobby, racing toward the door.

It was a relief, feeling the biting November air upon his face. He could still feel the man's bony fingers tightly gripping his arm. He shook his head, wanting to banish the horrifying feeling that still haunted him. His heart was pounding, his breath coming in gasps, but at least he was finally alone.

Back behind the theater, the rugged hills were completely deserted. Through the walls he could hear the crowd's thunderous applause. The play, the audience, even Miranda . . . suddenly it all seemed so far away.

All that mattered was that he was alone.

Leaning against the wall, he gazed out at the woods, finding there the serenity he sought. The forest stretched on forever. The towering cedars, proud and tall, rose up against the horizon, their fragrance permeating the air. High above was the winter sky, cold and bleak.

The forest. As always it beckoned to him. And as always its draw was powerful. His muscles twitched. He pricked his ears, already picking up the enticing sounds of small animals skittering across the forest floor, carpeted in decaying leaves and brittle evergreen needles.

He took a few steps closer to the edge. He yearned to race through the forest, luxuriating in the freedom, in his own power, in the knowledge that in this realm he was king. . . .

Suddenly his longing faded. He stiffened, aware that someone else, *something* else, was near.

The air changed. What had before been a bracing iciness quickly became almost intolerable. While only moments earlier the mountain air had smelled fresh and fragrant, it was now odious.

And then he saw them. In the woods, in a small clearing just inside the forest. A pair of animals, their movements studied yet graceful. Standing face-to-face, poised in a fighting stance, the tension between them so thick it was almost palpable.

Two wolves. One as white as the bright light of a full moon, the other as black as the winter sky.

Large. Powerful. Eyes glowing with a luminescence so bright, so eerie, it appeared to be rooted in otherworldliness.

Werewolves.

As he watched, spellbound, the black wolf made a move toward the white one. It was slightly larger than its opponent, its chest broader and more powerful. It bared its gigantic teeth as a savage snarl rose up from its throat. The white wolf, considerably more agile, recoiled slightly, not in fear but in preparation for its retaliation.

He knew instantly that this was to be a fight to the death.

Garth made a movement toward them. At the same time he was both fascinated and repelled, unable to resist the urge to get closer. To try to make sense of what was happening before his eyes. He walked slowly, taking silent steps until he was so close he could see the glistening of their sharp teeth.

And then, in an instant, they both vanished. The clearing was suddenly empty. Not a twig, not a blade of grass, had been disturbed. It appeared that nothing had happened.

Puzzled, he reached out his hand, trying to touch what he now knew had never really been there.

He was shaking. He looked around him, startled by the subtle changes he perceived. The air was no longer icy; once again it was only refreshingly brisk. The fresh scent of the cedars surrounded him, filling his nostrils with their pungent fragrance.

He was struck again by how alone he was. This time, the feeling filled him with terror.

He turned, dashing back to the building behind him. His mouth was dry.

"Miranda!" he cried in a hoarse whisper, grabbing for the handle of the door.

He leaned against its hard wooden surface after it closed behind him, shutting out the night. His eyes clamped shut, he waited to catch his breath. From inside the auditorium he once again heard the sound of applause, so loud, so thunderous it made the floor vibrate.

He headed down a corridor, toward the backstage area. He had to see her. He had to tell her.

Backstage, dozens of people were crowded around, their faces lit up with excitement, their voices loud. Anxiously he sought out Miranda. Finally he spotted her, standing in their midst. Her cheeks were pink, her dark eyes bright.

"Miranda." This time he simply mouthed the word, hoping she would sense his presence. Hoping she would come.

His plea was answered. Suddenly she was looking at him, her face softening into a smile.

"Garth!" she cried, reaching out her hand. "I'm so glad you're here. Come meet some of my friends!"

He made his way through the throng, seeing only her. "Miranda," he said once again. This time his voice was pleading. She was beaming as she took his hand. "Garth, this is Ann Stevens, the costume designer. She's the one responsible for all the magnificent costumes in the play."

"Only partly responsible," the woman said, smiling. "Miranda and the other actors get some of the credit for showing off my creations in their best light."

"Hello," Garth said politely, nodding in the

woman's direction. "Miranda, I have to talk to you. I—"

"And you remember Elinor, don't you?" Miranda had already moved away, dragging Garth with her. "Over here, Elinor!"

"Great job, Miranda!" She leaned over, giving Miranda a quick hug.

"Thanks. Did you notice I nearly flubbed my opening line in the second scene—"

"Miranda," Garth told her in a loud whisper, "I just saw something incredible. In the woods. I had a vision. A terrible vision—"

"Miranda, we have to talk about your entrance at the beginning of act two," someone interrupted. A man dressed in period costume had come over. He placed both hands on her shoulders. "Tonight you came *this* close to knocking my helmet off with your sword!"

Miranda let out a melodious laugh, a sound Garth didn't recognize. He glanced over at her, surprised.

All of a sudden he saw her in a different light. She was in her element here, among her friends. Confident, comfortable, flourishing in a way he'd never seen before.

"Miranda, come over here for a second! I want you to tell you an idea I had for a change in the final scene. . . ."

As she moved away from him, Garth felt more alone than he ever had before.

CHAPTER
8

Miranda lay stretched across her bed, her diary open to a blank page, her pen poised in midair. But rather than writing, she was spending her Saturday morning daydreaming. Wrapping a strand of dark hair around her finger, she leaned back against the bed and in her mind relived the evening before.

What an incredible experience! Standing up onstage, dressed in her fine costume, the thick dark red folds of velvet that transformed her into the seventeen-year-old French peasant girl whose great courage and determination saved her country from its archenemy. Reciting the lines of dialogue that after long weeks of rehearsal had started coming from her heart rather than simply from her memory. Knowing that out beyond the glaring footlights edging the stage sat a mesmerized audience. Feeling confident that through her words and her actions she was bringing them along with her on an exciting journey through time, through space . . . through imagination.

For those two hours, nothing else had existed, nothing else had mattered. All her day-to-day concerns had faded as she became totally absorbed in an experience that bordered on mystical. And now that she'd sampled something so wondrous, she wanted to keep it part of her life forever.

Yet as thrilling as it all was, she knew perfectly well the Pacific Players' production of *Saint Joan* wasn't going to run forever. In fact, there were only three performances left. The joy she'd been experiencing, her ecstasy over being part of a first-rate theatrical company, was destined to be short-lived. She let out a wistful sigh, then bent her head over her diary, determined to capture some of what she was feeling in her journal.

"Miranda?" The sound of her mother's voice from the doorway startled her.

"Yes, Mom?"

"There's a man here to see you."

"A man?"

"Look. He gave me his card."

Puzzled, Miranda leaped off the bed. She gasped.

"Robert Dolan," read the bold black letters printed on the white business card. Underneath, in slightly smaller print, was written, "Talent Scout."

Miranda gripped her mother's arm. "Is this a joke?"

"I don't think so, Miranda."

"What should I do?"

Her mother laughed. "How about coming downstairs and talking to him?"

Miranda was suddenly self-conscious. As she took a moment to run a comb through her wild mane of dark curly hair and brush on some blush, she studied the reflection in the mirror. *If only I'd had some notice!* she thought, panic rising from deep inside. *I would have washed my hair, bought myself a new outfit. . . .*

Letting out a sigh, she pulled three or four sweaters out of a drawer, picked out one in a pale shade of blue she'd been told was flattering, and wriggled into it.

After quickly glancing at her reflection one last time, she came down the stairs. She cleared her throat nervously, then stood as tall and as proudly as she could as she made her entrance. "Mr. Dolan?" She extended her hand as she came into the living room. "I'm Miranda Campbell."

"Yes, I know." Mr. Dolan rose from the couch, where he was sitting next to her mother. As he shook her hand, he looked at her appraisingly. "You're even prettier up close than onstage."

Miranda could feel her cheeks growing hot. "Please sit down."

Once he was settled onto the couch again, he studied Miranda for a few seconds more. Sitting in the soft upholstered chair, it was all she could do not to squirm, or grab one of the throw pillows and hide behind it. Somehow, she managed to sit still.

Robert Dolan leaned over the coffee table and picked up the program from *Saint Joan* that her mother had been keeping there. He opened it to the page containing the cast's biographical sketches.

"According to this, *Saint Joan* is the first play you've been in."

Miranda's heart sank. *I knew this was too good to be true,* she thought.

"I've done others, but they were school productions."

The man was silent for what seemed an eternity. And then he said, "Not a bad performance, considering."

"Thank you."

A long silence followed. "My goodness," Mrs. Campbell suddenly interjected with forced cheerfulness. "I haven't even offered you anything to drink. Would you like some coffee, Mr. Dolan?"

"No, thank you. I won't be staying long."

So he didn't like what he was seeing, Miranda thought, her heart sinking. True, he thought she was pretty. And obviously he'd been impressed by what he'd seen onstage. But the bottom line was that she was an amateur. Someone who'd put on a good performance but had no track record. Not the kind of person any reputable theater company would ever be willing to take a chance on. . . .

"I've been retained," Mr. Dolan said abruptly, "by the Limelight Theater Company in Portland. They want me to find a young woman to star in an experimental play they're currently casting."

Miranda glanced at her mother. The hopeful, expectant look on her face matched exactly what Miranda was feeling.

"The play was written by France's hottest new playwright. Limelight's the only theater company in America he'll allow to touch it. They need somebody good—but fresh—and they need her in a hurry."

Mr. Dolan tossed the program back onto the coffee table.

"Interested in auditioning?"

Miranda could hardly believe her ears. The Limelight Theater Company was one of the finest theatrical groups in the Pacific Northwest! She'd gone up to Portland to see their productions and had always been impressed.

She wanted to leap out of her chair, throw her arms around Mr. Dolan, and squeal, "Of *course* I'd love to audition!"

Instead she pretended to consider his invitation, hoping her pounding heart wouldn't give her away.

"The Limelight Theater Company?" she said slowly. And then, with all the dignity she could muster, she nodded her head and said, "That sounds like an extremely worthwhile opportunity. Yes, Mr. Dolan, I believe I would like to audition."

She was turning out to be an even better actress than she'd realized.

"I can't believe it!" Miranda exclaimed to her mother. The two of them sat at the dining-room table, both excited as they speculated about where Mr. Dolan's invitation might lead. "Being asked to audition for the Limelight Theater Company . . . It's a dream come true!"

"I'm so happy for you," said Mrs. Campbell. She leaned over and gently brushed back a strand of her daughter's hair. "You deserve it, honey."

When the doorbell sounded, she cast a wary look at her mother. "You don't suppose it's Mr. Dolan again, do you? Coming back to say he changed his mind?"

Mrs. Campbell just laughed.

When Miranda opened the front door she found Garth standing on the other side.

"Garth! Just the person I wanted to talk to!" She threw her arms around him. "You're not going to believe what happened! It's simply the best, the most amazing . . ."

The tension in his body caused her to draw back. She studied his face and saw that his expression was earnest.

"What's wrong?"

"Miranda, we have to talk."

"Hello, Garth. Nice to see you again." Mrs. Campbell poked her head into the front hallway. "Miranda, I'm going upstairs to make some calls."

Miranda led Garth into the living room.

"Oh, Garth, I just have to tell you what happened this morning!" She sank onto the couch next to him, her legs folded up underneath her. "A talent scout came by this morning!"

"A talent scout?"

She nodded. "Robert Dolan. He saw me in *Saint Joan.* He wants me to audition for the Limelight Theater Company in Portland!

"This is the most exciting thing that's ever happened to me. Mr. Dolan said somebody would be in touch with me sometime over the next few weeks, after he's had a chance to talk to the director at Limelight. . . ."

She sensed he was barely listening. "Garth?"

"I—I'm sorry, Miranda. It's wonderful news, and I'm really happy for you. It's just that I'm having trouble paying attention."

"You're really upset, aren't you?" She reached over and put her hand on his arm. "And here I am, babbling away. . . . What is it?"

Garth buried his head in his hands. "I tried

to tell you about it last night, after the play. But you were so busy. . . ."

A wave of guilt rushed over her. He had needed her, and she hadn't been there for him. Still, she'd been so exhilarated the evening before. The excitement of the play, the thrill of another successful performance, had made it difficult for her to concentrate on him.

"I'm not busy now." Earnestly she looked into his eyes. "Tell me, Garth. What happened?"

"A stranger approached me. A man. It was in the lobby of the theater. I had to get out, to get some air. And all of a sudden, he was there. He touched my shoulder—"

"What did he say?"

"I—I'm not sure. Something about wanting to help me."

Miranda frowned. "What could he possibly have meant by that?"

"I don't know. I ran away. He frightened me. Something about him seemed so intense, so desperate. . . .

"But that wasn't really what was troubling me." He hesitated before adding, "I—I had another vision last night."

Miranda took his hand in hers. "Tell me."

"It started during the play. When Joan of Arc is burned at the stake. I was feeling restless, and that man in the lobby made me feel uneasy, so I went outside to get some air. And there, out in the woods—"

"What was it?" Her voice was gentle. "What did you see?"

"Two wolves." He swallowed hard. "Two were-wolves."

She gripped his hand more tightly. "Go on. It's all right."

"One was black and one was white. They were huge, powerful animals, Miranda. Frightening in their size . . . and their intensity. I could feel their fury. Their rage. I got a sense that they were both willing to fight to the death." His voice trailed off for a moment, before he started up again.

"And then, as soon as I got close, they vanished. It wasn't until then that I realized they weren't real. The whole thing left me terrified. I had a sense that there was something monumental about the moment I witnessed . . . that there was something of momentous importance at stake. Perhaps even so great that it was beyond my comprehension.

"And," he went on, his voice strained, "I had a terrible feeling of foreboding. As if, somehow, it all had something to do with me. That I was involved . . ."

Miranda leaned over and hugged him, nestling her face into his neck. "My poor Garth. My poor, poor Garth."

They were silent for a long time before she

asked, "Do you have any idea what it means?"

"No. It's just one more piece in this crazy puzzle that doesn't make any sense at all."

"It does sound frightening. No wonder you're haunted by it. But there's one good thing about the visions you've been having."

He looked at her questioningly, his blue eyes clouded.

"Somebody—or something—is trying to communicate with you," said Miranda. "There's some force out there that's trying to help you understand."

After he'd left, Miranda went into her bedroom, closed the door, and lay down on her bed. Only this time, it wasn't a delicious reverie that had her so preoccupied.

It was her own confusion. She felt so torn! Here she was at a crossroads in her life, a period in which dreams she'd barely dared to dream up until now were suddenly coming true. Her success with the Pacific Players, the chance to work with an even more prominent acting company up in Portland . . .

But then there was her love for Garth. While part of her wanted to soar, to stretch far beyond anything she'd even been able to imagine, she felt as if she were being selfish.

He needed her.

There was something else nagging at her, a

feeling she was reluctant to acknowledge but which would not allow itself to stay suppressed much longer.

Fear.

Miranda was afraid. Only now was she beginning to understand the curse under which Garth lived. It was evil. All consuming. A terrible force whose power was rooted in the realm of the supernatural.

While part of her remained steadfast, determined to stick by Garth through whatever trials lay ahead, another part warned her to stay away.

This is dangerous, a knowing voice insisted. *Keep away. Look after yourself.*

You have no way of knowing what you're really dealing with.

CHAPTER 9

Miranda eased on the brakes of her bicycle as she turned a corner onto Moss Avenue, the main street of Norton. She was still troubled by what Garth had told her about his vision. She could see that he was in agony . . . but she was powerless to help. Then there was her excitement over Robert Dolan's visit. Yet the exhilaration she longed to feel struggled against the heaviness in her heart.

She needed a respite from ruminating about the complications of her relationship with Garth. She decided to focus on something more manageable: getting Elinor a special gift for her birthday. She was hoping the gesture might ease some of the tension still lingering between them. She intended to scour some of the more interesting shops in Overlook's neighboring town until she came up with something unique.

It was a sunny Saturday afternoon, and she was looking forward to an afternoon out. The town of Norton, three miles inland across a hilly country road, was much bigger than Overlook. Miranda always enjoyed browsing in the shops lining Moss Avenue, including an unusual card and gift emporium and a clothing boutique that she loved. Those two shops in particular were what she'd had in mind when she'd first planned this shopping spree.

Her father's veterinary office was also along that strip. After chaining her bike to a pole, she decided on impulse to stop in. Chances were good he'd be on the road, as many of his clients were farmers in the rich flatlands just beyond the craggy mountains that ran along the coast. Still, it was worth a try.

The waiting room of Dr. Campbell's bright, airy office was filled with the usual assortment of animals, accompanied by their concerned owners.

"Hi, Miranda!" the receptionist greeted her warmly. "Your dad's just finishing up with a patient. He'll be free in a minute."

Just then Dr. Campbell came striding into the waiting room, his white lab coat billowing out behind him.

"Miranda! What a nice surprise!" Her father turned to his next client, a boy of about twelve who was cradling a terrier puppy in his lap.

"Mike, why don't you bring Scooter into Room Two? I'll be with you in a minute."

Miranda plopped into a seat in the small room her father kept as his business office.

There were veterinary journals in uneven piles on the shelves lining one wall. Medical forms and other papers were strewn across his desk. He barely seemed aware of the clutter as he sat in his swivel chair.

"How are things going, sweetie?"

"Great, Dad." She swallowed hard. She hated holding back from her father. But she wanted to banish all the fears and other dark thoughts from her mind, and concentrate on the positive aspects of her life. "You'll never guess what happened this morning. A talent scout from a theater company in Portland came to the house!"

She went on to tell him all the details of the unexpected invitation to audition. She was so excited that the words spilled out. As she spoke, a big grin lit up her father's face.

"Oh, honey, that's wonderful. I'm so happy for you!"

"Thanks. Oh, Daddy, it's like a dream come true! I never in a million years expected something like this to happen!"

"If there's one thing I've learned, it's that things don't always turn out the way we expect." There was a look of sadness in his eyes.

A few minutes later, Miranda was heading

down Moss Avenue, carrying the canvas shopping bag she'd tucked into her wicker bicycle basket. She was about to go into the clothing boutique when she noticed a sign tacked to a telephone pole. LOOKING FOR THE UNUSUAL? it read. Underneath was an arrow.

Miranda took a few steps in the direction of the arrow. She found herself standing on the corner. To her left was a small side street, one to which she'd never before paid much attention. She headed down it, checking the signs over the few shops on it.

She knew when she'd reached the right one. It was narrow, easy to miss, as its doorway was set back from the sidewalk by five or six feet. A faded sign was nailed over the front, the shop's name written in plain black letters: "Et Cetera." And underneath, in smaller letters: "Oddities, Antiquities, and Other Glorious Junque."

Curious, Miranda pulled open the door. The air was stale and thick with dust. Within seconds her eyes and nose began to sting.

The shop was so poorly lit that it took her eyes a few seconds to adjust. Then, slowly, she began to make out what was before her. Her eyes widened as she saw that inside the cramped space was the most amazing array of memorabilia she had ever seen.

The store looked like a place in which time had stood still—or at least gotten so mixed up it was impossible to tell exactly when it was. Unusual pieces, some beautiful, others bizarre, covered every available inch of the store. Piled onto the seat of a wooden rocking chair were several well-worn quilts; draped along the back of it was a long red feather boa. Lined up on shelves was an eclectic assortment of trinkets: a ceramic cookie jar shaped like a clown; a chubby Buddha made of brass; and a plastic black cat that was a clock, its eyes moving back and forth as it marked off each passing second.

To the right was a metal clothing rack, so crowded that the row of garments was bulging and the hangers crisscrossed over one another. Hanging on one end was a wedding gown. It was made of cream-colored lace that looked wilted, the twenty or thirty tiny buttons that ran up the back covered in fraying satin. Behind it was a black velvet cape, lined with royal-blue silk. Just beyond that was a 1950's-style cocktail dress, a shiny kelly-green fabric cut in a sheath style with a draped off-the-shoulder neckline.

Along a shelf that hung just above the rack were all kinds of hats: a straw hat with a red band, a pink bonnet edged with jaunty sprigs of flowers, a dramatic velveteen creation with a veil in front and feathers in the back. Tossed among them were shoes, delicate dancing slippers, chunky cowboy boots, even a Turkish-style pair with toes that curled up.

Miranda was studying the various pieces

hanging on the wall—an antique mirror in an
ornate frame, some framed posters from World
War II encouraging civilians to buy war bonds—
when a noise behind her caused her to start.

"Can I help you?"

She whirled around, spying an old man shuf-
fling toward her from the back of the store,
which was separated from the front by a tattered
shawl tacked up in a doorway. The man looked
as though he was in his seventies—balding,
stooped over, moving slowly. Clearly, he was
dressed in finds from his own inventory.

Yet what struck her most was his eyes. Even in
the dim light of the shop Miranda could see
that they were bright and alert. Something
about the look in them implied that he knew a
secret no one else knew.

"I'm looking forsomething . . . unusual."

The old man smiled. "Then you've definitely
come to the right place. Is this for yourself?"

"No, for a friend. It's her birthday."

Miranda hadn't even realized she'd grown
quiet until the man startled her by saying, "Ah.
Things are not so good between you two. You're
hoping to find a special present that will smooth
over some hard feelings."

"H-how did you know?"

"It's written all over your face." The old man
was headed toward the back corner of the store.
Tucked away behind an old-fashioned gramo-

phone was a glass display case, covered in dust. The man reached into his pocket, pulled out a linen handkerchief, and cleared away the grimy layer. "Perhaps there's something here?"

Miranda leaned over the display case. Strewn haphazardly across the top shelf were pieces of jewelry—rings, charm bracelets, cameo pins edged with intricate gold filigree. There were other small trinkets, as well: a silver comb and brush set, a venetian-glass paperweight, a Wedgwood box. She was poring over them, carefully considering each one, when one piece in particular caught her eye.

It was a tiny picture frame, smaller than the palm of her hand. The opening was an oval; around the perimeter were fanciful curlicues. The brass was badly tarnished, yet Miranda could see it was a handsome, well-made piece.

"That picture frame—"

"It's a beauty, isn't it?" The old man was already reaching behind the glass case to remove it. "I can see you've got a good eye."

Holding it in her hand, Miranda knew it was the perfect present for Elinor. After glancing at the price tag hanging from it, she said, "I'll take it."

She was about to turn away when she noticed something else. It was on the bottom shelf of the display case, tossed in among a handful of other items that the proprietor must have thought would never sell, things like a single earring, missing its mate, and a glass paperweight with a large chip in one side.

At first she thought it was a letter opener. When she crouched down to study it more carefully, however, she saw its blade was extremely sharp. It was a knife—but a knife unlike any other she'd ever seen. The handle was made of wood, clearly hand-carved by a skilled craftsperson.

At first the complicated design looked abstract. Upon closer examination, Miranda made out the heads of two animals face to face. One snarling, the other simply staring.

Wolves' heads.

"Could I see that?" she asked on impulse.

The old man seemed surprised. "The knife?"

"It's interesting, don't you think?"

"Very interesting." He cast her an odd look as he handed it to her. He was handling it cautiously. "It's also very sharp, so be careful. Could be dangerous."

Miranda laid it on top of the glass case. It was beautiful—and at the same time sinister. A part of her told her she should forget she'd ever seen it. But another part of her was drawn to it in a way she couldn't explain.

"This looks handmade," she said.

"No doubt."

"Is it Native American?"

"Could be. The truth is, I don't remember how it came to be in the shop. It's just been sitting here, waiting, for the longest time."

"How much is it?" she asked, running her finger along the handle. The unevenness of the carved surface was an odd sensation.

"Let me see." The old man glanced at the price tag dangling from the bottom. "Fifty dollars."

"Fifty dollars! That's too much. Thank you, but I can't—"

"Now, hold on." The man frowned. "Seems to me this has been sitting in that case, gathering dust, for long enough. If you're really interested . . . well, I'll let you have it for twenty."

The price was still a bit higher than what Miranda wanted to spend, but she couldn't leave it. After the man wrapped it in thick layers of tissue paper, she tucked the knife into the bottom of her bag. She liked the feel of it, a nice solid weight that wasn't too heavy.

"Don't forget what I said, now," the man called after her as she turned to leave the shop. "Be careful with that. Could be very dangerous."

When Miranda stepped out of the shop, she discovered that darkness had already swallowed up the November day. An icy wind cut into her as she headed up the tiny side street.

As she walked, the knife at the bottom of her bag began to feel strangely heavy. With each step it weighed down her bag a bit more. Suddenly she was anxious to put it into the wicker basket of her bicycle.

She started as she turned the corner. Someone was lurking near her bike. It took only a few seconds to recognize the shadowy figure.

"Featherwoman?"

The old woman glanced up. Her face was illuminated by the streetlight above. Every wrinkle in her brown skin was highlighted, the lines running along her cheeks and forehead as pronounced as the deep crevices that snake across the parched desert floor. At that moment, Miranda almost believed the rumors that she was more than a hundred years old.

Her piercing jet-black eyes were a sharp contrast. They were shining in the glaring light of the streetlamp, reflecting the light in such a way as to appear they were emitting light of their own.

Miranda didn't hide her surprise. "Were you looking for me?"

Featherwoman acted as if she hadn't heard. "You have taken an important step, my child."

She spoke so softly that it took Miranda a few seconds to make sense of what she'd said. And even when she'd understood the words, she didn't comprehend their meaning.

"Excuse me?"

"It is the way it must be," the old woman went on, her eyes burning into Miranda's. "What has been set in motion cannot be stopped."

Miranda opened her mouth, once again intending to ask the meaning of Featherwoman's puzzling words. But she stopped herself. As she peered at her more closely, she saw that the woman looked as if she were in a trance.

Miranda wondered if she even knew what she was saying.

"Uh, I'd better be going," she said, suddenly uncomfortable. "It's getting late, and—"

"It is your destiny," Featherwoman said in a hoarse whisper. "You are following the path that has been prescribed for you."

Miranda had already unchained her bicycle and was wheeling it away, grasping the handles tightly. She didn't want to look as if she were running away, yet the impulse to flee was too strong to ignore.

She doesn't know what she's saying, Miranda thought wildly. She's just rambling on and on, without having any idea . . .

"The knife. It is now in your possession. This is as it must be."

Featherwoman's words stopped Miranda dead in her tracks. A chill ran through her.

She whirled around, her bicycle nearly toppling over. "What did you say?"

But the old woman simply stared, her eyes as black as coals and burning with the same intensity. And then she turned away, disappearing into the night as silently and as unexpectedly as she had come.

CHAPTER
10

Miranda was still shaken by her encounter with Featherwoman as she careened into Overlook on her bicycle. She tried to put the entire incident out of her mind, telling herself that running into the old woman had simply been a coincidence . . . and that the odd words she had spoken were nothing more than confused ramblings.

Wanting to take her mind off the disturbing incident, she decided to stop at Corinne's house. She'd wanted to visit her for some time, hoping that somehow the fact that she was concerned about her friend would permeate the protective cloak Corinne had pulled around herself ever since the night of the attack. She veered off the main road, opting for a back route that took her right past the Davises' house. The lights shining from the windows were inviting, offering a chance to put the eerie incident in Norton behind her.

"I hope this isn't a bad time," Miranda said politely, once Corinne's mother answered the door.

"Not at all, Miranda." Mrs. Davis looked disoriented, as if she had yet to grasp the jarring events of the past weeks. "Thank you for coming."

"How is she, Mrs. Davis?" Miranda searched the woman's face anxiously. She was hoping to see some sign of optimism. Instead, what she saw in the tired gray eyes and the tense, down-turned lips was sadness. Sadness—and fear.

"I hardly know her anymore." Mrs. Davis tried to force a laugh, without much success. "It's as if she's a stranger. My own daughter. I look right into her eyes and she doesn't even recognize me."

"She's suffered a terrible trauma," Miranda reminded her gently.

Mrs. Davis's face suddenly became animated. "Yes, but what was it? No one knows! Nobody can tell me, not the police, not the doctors. . . ." There was bitterness in her tone. "My poor baby has scratches all over her body. Scratches . . . and teeth marks."

"They're saying there's a crazed animal running around the outskirts of Overlook." Miranda tried to keep her tone even.

Mrs. Davis didn't seem to have heard. She was shaking her head slowly, staring off without seeming to focus on anything in particular. "They tell me it's a miracle she's alive. But she hardly seems alive at all. My little girl."

"Give it time," Miranda said gently, placing her hand on Mrs. Davis's arm. "The doctors say she's doing very well. Just be a little patient."

Suddenly Mrs. Davis reached over, putting her hand over Miranda's. "You're a good girl, Miranda," she said. "You've always been such a good friend to my Corinne."

Miranda lowered her eyes.

"I'll take you in now," Mrs. Davis offered.

The curtains in the bedroom were tightly drawn. The only illumination came from a tiny night-light shaped like a seashell, casting huge, oddly shaped shadows against the walls and ceiling. Corinne was sitting up in bed, staring straight ahead. Her shoulder-length blond hair had been carefully brushed and pulled back into a neat ponytail. Clasped tightly against her chest was a tattered teddy bear.

"Hello, Corinne," Miranda said in a soft voice.

"She can't hear you," Mrs. Davis insisted.

"We don't know that for certain." Miranda went over to the bed, taking small steps. "It's me, Corinne. Miranda. I came to visit you. I've been very worried about you, and I wanted to make sure you were all right."

Corinne just stared straight ahead. Miranda leaned forward, looking into her face, squinting as she studied her in the dim light. Her blue eyes were hollow, seeing nothing, knowing nothing, understanding nothing.

The horror of the entire situation suddenly rushed over Miranda. The terrible curse that plagued Garth was responsible for this. The evil, inexplicable power that controlled him, taking hold, turning him into something almost as evil as itself . . .

And she, through her love for Garth, was also involved.

All of a sudden Miranda clasped Corinne by the shoulders, burying her face against her neck.

"Oh, Corinne!" she sobbed. "Please, *please*, be all right!"

Standing in front of the mirror hanging above her dresser, Miranda picked up her hairbrush and slowly pulled it through her thick mane of dark wavy hair, its red highlights glinting. It was Saturday evening, right after dinner, and she was getting ready for Bobby's party. Yet as she stared at her reflection, studying the dress she'd decided to wear, crushed velvet in a deep shade of gold, her thoughts drifted.

She found herself ruminating about how strange it was that she was going to be just another guest at his party. And that she was going with Garth, while Bobby's date for the evening would be Amy. Miranda and Bobby had been together for so long, sharing so many experiences, making plans . . .

She stopped fussing with her hair, putting her brush down as a knot formed in her stomach. There were so many shifts in her life, so many changes. She sometimes wondered how she would ever get through them all, creating a brand-new sense of order as she moved on.

Taking a deep breath, she picked up her jewelry box, forcing herself to push her anxieties out of her mind. She longed to forget about the things that were plaguing her, at least for a little while. An evening out was exactly what she needed, she thought as she put on a pair of silver Native American earrings, checking her reflection to make certain they were just right. And it would be great seeing the crowd from school. Between rehearsing for the play and being with Garth, she hadn't had much time for socializing lately. She was looking forward to a long, relaxing night of listening to music, dancing, and catching up on the latest gossip. When a nagging fear arose, a question about whether she would still feel comfortable with the group now that her own life seemed to be veering off in such a different direction, she quickly dismissed it.

Still, she had to admit she was a little nervous. This would be the first time she'd be introducing Garth into her circle of friends. He'd met a handful of them at the Homecoming

Dance a few weeks earlier, but that was before
the attacks on the two students from her high
school. Before the ugly rumors had sprung up,
speculating that the sudden acts of violence
might be related to the appearance of a new-
comer in town.

Still staring into the mirror but no longer
seeing, Miranda replayed in her mind a scene
she'd been keeping tucked away. It was right
after the memorial service for Andy Swensen,
the Overlook High School senior who'd been
mauled in the woods the night of the dance.
Selina and Corinne had sought her out at her
locker, claiming they simply wanted to update
her on the latest gossip.

"It's that new boyfriend of yours," Corinne
had told her.

"The whole school is buzzing about him,"
Selina had continued. "But nobody knows a
thing about him. And you're being so secretive.
It all seems kind of . . . weird."

It was Corinne who'd finally come right out
with it. "Some of the kids are joking about how
this mystery man of yours took you on a date in
the woods—to hunt for dead bodies." Her blue
eyes had narrowed as she'd added, "Some people think he might have had something to do
with Andy's death. He is a stranger, after all. He
just appeared from out of nowhere."

As much as Miranda hated to admit it, Corinne's accusations had precipitated her own doubts about Garth. It wasn't the first time she'd found herself wondering about his mystery.

Now, of course, it all made sense. Nevertheless, she was living every minute of her life with an oppressive burden: having to remain cloaked in secretiveness. It was disturbing, having to keep silent. Yet she knew she had no choice but to protect Garth. There was simply no other way.

Suddenly wanting to push all that aside, Miranda turned her attention to the birthday present she'd bought Elinor, sitting on the dresser. She and Garth had arranged to meet outside Bobby's house later that evening so she could drop it off at Elinor's house before the party. The picture frame was in a box, wrapped in pretty paper and tied with a bow. She hoped Elinor would like it. Even more, she hoped she'd appreciate the sentiments behind it.

Thinking about Elinor's gift reminded Miranda of her other purchase from the strange shop in Norton. After glancing at the doorway of her bedroom to make sure her mother was nowhere in sight, she opened the top drawer of her dresser. There, tucked in among the makeup and the bottles of perfume, was the knife.

She held it up to the light and examined it. The blade was scratched, the metal not as shiny as it had probably once been. But it was the handle that was so remarkable. Two wolves, eye to eye, carved into the soft wood. Their expressions were angry, menacing . . . cruel. Even though it was crafted simply and somewhat crudely, the two animals were remarkably lifelike.

It was strange, the way she'd run into Featherwoman right after she'd found the knife in that strange shop in Norton, a store she'd never noticed before. She wondered how the old Native American woman had known about it. Perhaps she'd peeked into the shop and seen her buying it. Yes, Miranda concluded, that was the only reasonable explanation.

Still, as she held the knife in her hands, an odd sensation came over her. She suddenly felt a prickling at the back of her neck, as if someone were standing right behind her.

She whirled around, so abruptly that the knife slid from her hand. There was no one there.

"Miranda!" Mrs. Campbell called upstairs from the living room.

She could hear her mother's tread on the stairs. Quickly she retrieved the knife from the floor. She glanced around the room, suddenly desperate to hide it.

"Miranda, I want you to tell me if this blouse looks all right with this skirt."

Her mother was almost up the stairs. Desperately Miranda flung open the door of her closet. At the bottom, in the very back corner, was a cardboard box, filled with old shoes and clothes that no longer fit.

"Give me your honest opinion."

Miranda crouched down only long enough to thrust the knife deep inside the box. By the time her mother appeared in the doorway, the closet door was closed and Miranda was standing in front of the mirror again, hairbrush in hand.

"Those look great together," she said, glancing over her shoulder. "Going out tonight?"

Mrs. Campbell nodded, a flush rising on her cheeks.

Suddenly a wave of understanding washed over Miranda. "You've got a date, haven't you? A date with Daddy."

Her mother laughed. "I know it probably sounds crazy to you. . . ."

"It doesn't sound crazy at all. I think it's wonderful."

"Me, too." Mrs. Campbell came over to her daughter and put her arms around her. "I guess we never really know where life is going to take us, do we?"

"No," Miranda agreed. As she returned her hug, she was thinking that her mother's words were truer than she knew.

Miranda arrived at the Clays' home to find it all decked out for a celebration. There was a stack of presents in the living room, and the dining room was festooned with crepe-paper streamers and clusters of colorful balloons. Delicious smells wafted from the kitchen. She was struck by what a happy place it was, especially compared to the somberness that hung over her own house lately.

More than twenty of Elinor's relatives had gathered for the birthday dinner. After Elinor introduced her around, the two girls ducked into the den.

"Miranda!" Elinor looked genuinely pleased to see her. "I thought you'd said you were going to a party tonight."

Miranda nodded. "I'm meeting Garth in half an hour. But I wanted to wish you a happy birthday in person."

"Thanks."

"Besides, you didn't think I'd let your birthday go by without giving you a present, did you?" With great ceremony Miranda reached into her purse, then handed over the small package.

"I guess I should be polite and say 'You shouldn't have.'" Elinor shrugged. "But to be perfectly honest, I'm really glad you did!"

Laughing, Miranda said, "Why don't you open it?"

Eagerly Elinor tore into the paper. When she took the brass picture frame out of its tissue, she let out a squeal.

"Oh, Miranda! It's gorgeous! Thank you so much."

"It was important to me that I help you celebrate." She paused before adding, "I've got something to celebrate, too."

"What?"

"I've been invited to audition for the Limelight Theater Company in Portland."

"That's *fabulous*!" Elinor shrieked. "Tell me every single detail!"

Miranda told her all about the visit from the talent scout. As she spoke, she realized how anxious she'd been to share the news with Elinor. After all, she'd been the one who'd supported her all through her audition for *Saint Joan*, as well as at all the rehearsals, up through opening night. She'd proven to be a sincere and caring friend—exactly the kind of person who would rejoice in Miranda's success, making it that much more meaningful.

"Oh, Miranda," Elinor breathed when she'd finished. "This is so great. Congratulations!"

"Actually, I was wondering if—"

"Yes?"

"If you'd be willing to drive to Portland with me when I go up for the audition." Suddenly shy, Miranda added, "I could use the moral support. Besides, it'd make it even more fun."

Elinor broke into a wide smile. "I'd love to!"

She leaned over and gave her a big hug.

When she drew away, her hazel eyes were shining.

"I'm really glad you stopped by, Miranda. And thanks again for the present."

"I'm glad you like it."

"I absolutely love it. And do you know what I'm going to use it for? I'm going to get my father to take a picture of you and me together. Let's go ask him."

"Wait a minute." Miranda placed her hand on Elinor's arm. "Elinor, did you talk to the police?"

"Yeah. I went this morning and filed a report."

"What did they say?"

"The officer I talked to wasn't directly involved in the case. He said he'd pass it on to somebody named Officer Vale."

"I know her," said Miranda. "She's in charge of the investigation of the recent attacks." She thought for a moment before saying, "Anyway, it's all behind us now. Can we just move on and forget about it?"

"Of course."

"Good. I don't want it to stand in our way."

A look of confusion crossed Elinor's face. But after a moment's pause, she simply shook her head. "It's forgotten, Miranda. The last thing I want is for anything to get in the way of our friendship.

"Now let's go back into the living room. My

dad's a real camera freak, and I'm sure he'll be thrilled to hear he's got two willing victims!"

Garth was waiting on the corner outside Bobby's house, just as he and Miranda had planned. He was standing in the dark, his hands thrust deep into the pockets of his gray suede jacket. He was under a streetlight, and his face was illuminated in such a way that it seemed to be glowing. The mass of blond curls on his head was disheveled, and his blue eyes were shining even in the dim light. Watching him, Miranda's heart felt as if it were being folded in half.

"Garth?" she called softly.

"Miranda." His face relaxed into a gentle smile. "I'm a little nervous about tonight," he confessed as she grew near.

"Don't be. We'll be together," she said, not revealing her own apprehensions.

He put his arms around her, drawing her close. His kiss was tender. She could feel herself relaxing as her body melted against his. Even the harshness of the cold November night faded. For the moment, there was only him.

The party was already in full swing by the time Miranda and Garth reached Bobby's house. Loud music was blaring as she led him inside. The entire first floor was filled with people talking and laughing. Off in one corner, a small group was dancing. Dawn Curley, dancing with a boy

Miranda recognized as a junior, gave her a big wave.

"Hey, Miranda. You made it." Bobby caught her eye as soon as she walked in. He came over to her, a can of Coke in his hand. For a moment, she thought he was going to lean over and kiss her hello. Instead, he took a sip of soda.

He glanced over at Garth, standing close at her side. "You must be Garth."

As the two boys shook hands, Garth said, "Thanks for inviting me."

"It looks like a great party," Miranda commented, glancing around.

"I'm glad you came," said Bobby. "I was afraid—"

"Well, well, well. If it isn't Overlook's number-one couple." Amy had just come over. She slung her arm around Bobby's waist, meanwhile looking Garth up and down through narrowed eyes. "So this is the famous Garth Gautier."

"And you are . . . ?" he asked politely.

"Amy Patterson." She tossed her head, her long blond locks dramatically catching the light. "You've created quite a stir around this town."

"Have I, Amy?"

The tension was so thick Miranda was growing uncomfortable. Nervously she glanced at Garth, anxious to see his reaction. He simply looked amused.

Bobby glanced from Amy to Garth, then

back to Amy. "Hey, how about a dance, Amy? I love this song."

She acted as if she hadn't heard. "Some of us think there's something mysterious about you, Garth Gautier. Something . . . shall we say, secretive?"

Garth's expression had grown more somber, the muscles around his mouth growing taut.

Selina came over then, munching on a handful of potato chips. She froze when she saw Miranda and Garth, her face suddenly tense. "Hello, Miranda." Glancing at Garth, she said, "Remember me? I'm Selina Lamont. We met at the Homecoming Dance."

Before he had a chance to reply, Amy said, "I was just telling Garth some of the rumors circulating around town, Selina. About how mysterious he is and all."

"Come on, Amy," Bobby said gently. "This is a party, remember? It's supposed to be fun."

"Oh, I'm having fun. I'm having lots of fun." Amy's blue eyes were still fixed coolly on Garth. "So are you going to spill your secrets? Who you are, where you came from, what you're doing here . . ."

"Garth," Miranda said, her voice strained, "maybe we should go get something to drink."

"There's something else we've all been wondering about." Amy cast Selina a meaningful look. "Go ahead, Selina. Ask him."

A look of alarm crossed Selina's face. "Ask him what?"

"You know. About the attacks. Tell him about the theory you and Corinne came up with. It's very interesting."

Miranda started. "What theory?"

"I'm sure you'll find it fascinating, Miranda," said Amy. Cocking her head toward Selina, she insisted, "Tell us."

Nervously Selina looked from Amy to Miranda, then back at Amy. "Only that it was kind of an odd coincidence that the attacks on the two students from our school occurred right after Garth came to town.

"I'm hardly the only one who noticed!" she added defensively, casting Miranda a pleading look. "Rumors have been flying for weeks. You already knew that, Miranda!"

But Miranda wasn't interested in Selina. She looked over at Garth. His entire body was stiff, his face hardened.

"Then there was that incident on your property," Amy went on, her voice growing even colder. "Poor Mark O'Neill, in the hospital with second-degree burns. And to think the bizarre 'accident' happened right outside Cedar Crest!"

"Hey, here's Tommy," Bobby suddenly said with forced enthusiasm as Tommy Devlin, Selina's boyfriend, appeared. "Tommy, why don't you and Selina dance? Come on, Amy. I don't want to stand around all night, yakking away."

He cast Miranda an apologetic look. She was relieved when he dragged Amy away by the arm, ignoring her protests. Tommy picked up on his desperation and followed suit.

Once they were alone, Miranda turned to Garth. "Maybe we should dance, too."

"Miranda." His blue eyes were clouded. "I think I'd better go."

"Garth, don't let Amy drive you away. She's not worth it. As for Selina . . ." Sadly she searched the room, seeking her out. She felt a pang of dismay as she watched Selina allowing herself to be dragged into a corner by Amy, who was whispering in her ear.

"I had no idea my coming here tonight would cause so many problems."

"My friends aren't all like them." Once again her eyes traveled around the room, looking for one of her other acquaintances from school, a face she could be certain would be friendly. She knew Dawn, of course, and she'd spotted Laura over in the corner, talking. . . . Yet she realized there was no one here she could count on one hundred percent. Of everyone she knew, only Elinor had proven to be a true friend.

Suddenly she, too, felt alienated from the group at the party.

"Why don't we both leave, Garth? We could go to Cedar Crest and—"

"No, Miranda. You stay. I'm going, but I want you to be with your friends. Please!"

"I want to be with you!"

"I don't belong in your life. Can't you see that?"

"But I don't care about them, Garth! I care about you!"

She didn't know if he'd heard. He had already turned toward the door, skirting a crowd that was laughing uproariously.

CHAPTER
11

As Miranda stepped out of Bobby's house, the night felt darker and colder than before. She glanced up at the sky and saw it was pitch-black, with dark rain clouds smothering the moon and the stars. She pulled her jacket more tightly around her, bracing herself against the bitter November air.

Tears stung her eyes, making it difficult for her to see clearly. It occurred to her that she should call her mother to ask for a ride home, but she was anxious to be out in the clear icy air, hoping a brisk walk home would help her calm down. Taking long strides, she headed out into the night. She kept her eyes down, concentrating on the events of the evening.

She'd stayed at the party another hour, talking to Laura and Dawn and some of her other acquaintances from school, determined to enjoy

herself. She wasn't surprised when that proved
impossible; both her anger at Garth and her re-
sentment toward her friends gnawed at her all
evening. Finally she'd snuck out without saying
good-bye. All she wanted was to get away. To be
alone. To find a way of quelling the storm of
emotions raging inside.

On impulse Miranda headed into the forest,
still lost in thought as she veered off the main
road into the dense growth. To most of the residents of Overlook, the woods had become a forbidding place, the scene of the recent attacks. Yet
she knew she had nothing to fear. In fact, in here
she expected to find the comfort she was seeking.

Almost immediately she felt more peaceful.
The piney fragrance of the tall cedars made the
air even more invigorating. The ground was a
carpet of moss, soft and spongy beneath her
feet. A heavy silence hung overhead, broken
only occasionally by the sound of a squirrel
scampering away or an owl taking flight.

Miranda was aware of the beauty of her surroundings as she made her way through the
woods, taking care not to stumble as she stepped
over a tangle of vines or jumped over a boggy
spot. Still, she was too drained to appreciate it.
Over and over in her mind, she replayed the
scene from the party.

She was deep inside the forest, not yet
halfway through, when the sky directly above

her resounded with a menacing rumble. The storm that had been brewing for the past hour was now threatening to erupt. She shuddered, feeling vulnerable and alone for the first time. Usually she felt so much at home on her own in the forest. All of a sudden the feeling of isolation seemed dangerous.

A flash of lightning lit up the forest. The shapes of the trees—their twisted black trunks, their gnarled branches stretching out in odd formations—jumped up all around her. Low bushes that looked like hunched-over gnomes surrounded her ominously. Everywhere there were dark shadows: deep, empty, mysterious.

"It's only a thunderstorm," Miranda said aloud, wanting to reassure herself.

Just then a loud crack of thunder made her jump. Instinctively she broke into a run, catching her foot in a clump of vines. She cried out, falling to the ground before she could catch herself.

It was only when she tried to stand up that she realized she'd twisted her ankle. It didn't feel broken; she decided it was probably just a minor sprain. She rubbed it hard, knowing it would take a few minutes before she was able to put her full weight on it—and knowing she would have to make her way home carefully.

More lightning flashed, once again illuminating the twisted trees. Their clawlike branches reached for her. Again she was surrounded by shadows, shadows in which anything or anyone might be lurking. . . .

"Don't be silly," she scolded herself aloud, massaging her ankle. "There's nothing to be afraid of. The scariest thing around is probably some old jackrabbit—and he'd be more afraid of me than I'd be of him."

Still, she glanced around nervously, her ears pricking up at the slightest sound. The rain had not yet begun to fall, but she was dreading the inevitable downpour. The thunder and lightning continued; the storm was close. If she didn't get going, she would no doubt get soaked.

A particularly loud clap of thunder sent her scrambling to her feet. The urge to flee this place was strong enough to prompt her to try putting her weight on her ankle. She let out a little cry, but it was rooted more in fear than in pain. She could walk. Her foot was sore and it would be slow going, but she could make it.

And then she heard a low rumbling sound.

At first she thought it was thunder.

But it was too loud, too terrible. The entire earth seemed to tremble. Miranda clamped her hands over her ears. The gesture did nothing to drown out the noise.

She realized then that the noise was not coming from above. It was coming from below.

Panic rose up inside her. Perhaps it was an earthquake, she reasoned, racking her brain for some piece of information, tucked away somewhere in the back of her mind, about the safest thing to do.

Instinctively she knew it was not an earthquake.

The thundering pounded through her head. She could no longer think. She shut her eyes, wanting only to escape.

It was then she began to cough, her closed eyes tearing and her nose stinging, her entire body rebelling against the repulsive odor that was burning her nostrils.

She had never before smelled anything so vile.

A bright flash of lightning prompted her to open her eyes. Instantly they grew wide—wide with surprise, wide with disbelief—above all, wide with fear.

Standing before her were three dark horsemen. They sat on formidable black beasts, horses much larger than any Miranda had ever seen. The animals' eyes were cold and unseeing, their legs massive, the muscles of their brawny chests bulging. They snorted loudly, stamping their huge hooved feet.

The men astride them were dressed entirely in black. They, too, were large, their shoulders broad and powerful. All three wore dark, heavy cloaks.

She was afraid to look up into their faces. When she finally forced herself to, she saw that she couldn't; the hoods of their cloaks covered them.

Beneath the fabric, there were only shadows.

She stood frozen to the spot. She wanted to run, but did not. It was not only the soreness of her ankle or her fear that kept her frozen.

She was mesmerized. Entranced, somehow, unable to run away even though what she confronted was horrible. At the same time it was fascinating, so bizarre that she could not take her eyes off the vision.

And then the horseman in the middle spoke. "Miranda," he said, his voice hoarse and low.

Her blood ran cold.

It knows my name, she thought.

Yet a small part of her wasn't surprised. Something inside had known all along that they'd come for her. To speak with her.

She could feel their power. It bore down on her, almost a physical force.

She lifted her face to them, waiting. Her fear was still great. Yet even while in its grip, she recognized that she was their captive. That she was enslaved by them. Above all, that she was powerless to resist.

He sensed danger.

He was alone at Cedar Crest. Watching the clock. Counting the hours. Regretting the tension that had hovered between Miranda and him as they parted. Above all longing for the time when they would once again be together, when everything could be smoothed over and their love could be reaffirmed.

He'd been home only a short time. The rest of the night stretched ahead, seemingly endless. The sky was black, swollen with menacing clouds. He stood at the window, looking out at the dark sky. And worrying about her.

He had no regrets about leaving the party. He didn't belong with those people. He wished she had come with him, that she were here now. . . .

Still, he did not begrudge her her freedom. And so he stayed in the shadows, waiting.

Suddenly a feeling of doom came over him. As he stood by the window, marveling over the great claps of thunder and the bright bursts of lightning that lit up the forbidding night, fear gripped him. His stomach lurched, the terror rooting itself there.

In an instant every one of his senses was on alert. Pure instinct took over.

Something was wrong. Miranda was in trouble.

He didn't remember leaving the house. All he knew was that suddenly he was tearing down Winding Way, the terrible fear sending bursts of adrenaline through his veins. He felt no fatigue as he ran. He was in a race—one in which his opponent was time.

He knew the danger was in the forest.

He pushed as hard as he could, his muscles beginning to ache as he ran. He lengthened his stride, forcing his legs to go faster and faster. His lungs hurt, rebelling against the formidable demands he was putting on them. His breaths came as gasps. He threw back his head and sucked in the air, desperate to keep going, desperate to go even faster.

He knew precisely where to go, as if some mystical part of himself sensed what the logical part could not. He was overwhelmed with terror that he was not going fast enough to reach her in time.

Once again he threw back his head, expecting to let out a cry of frustration. Of pain. Perhaps even of defeat.

Instead, the sound that escaped his lips was not that of a man. It was the howl of a wolf.

He realized then that he had changed into a werewolf. The same process as the night of the fire had occurred once again, the shapeshifting coming upon him spontaneously, so quickly, he didn't even feel it until it was complete. His chest had grown to massive proportions, his limbs had stretched out long and lean. His clothes had been torn away from his body, falling to the ground as he sped through the forest. Golden fur covered his flesh. His head had also been reshaped: his jaw had lengthened, his ears had been transformed, his teeth had grown large and sharp.

He was now an animal. Yet just as the other

time he had shapeshifted without warning, the separation of man and beast was vague. While he was operating largely on instinct, relying more on his senses than on his mind, his thoughts remained those of a human being.

Once again, the man and the werewolf were one. Both spirits coexisted in the same body. And both were determined, combining their energies in such a way that no person, no thing, could possibly defeat them.

She felt hypnotized.

Miranda stood before the three horsemen without moving. Yes, she felt the terror. It was a physical presence with a life of its own. It held her in its icy grasp, freezing her blood, immobilizing every muscle, pulling all her nerves taut. Meanwhile a small voice deep inside screamed at her, telling her to run, to get away while she still could.

Yet there was something else. Something intriguing about their power. Something inviting.

Something irresistible.

"Miranda," said the horseman in the center, "come with us."

Then the second one spoke, his voice similarly low and rasping. "Miranda, you belong with us."

And then the third: "You are one of ours."

She hesitated, feeling their power.

And then, slowly, with one arm outstretched,

she took a hesitant step toward them.

Suddenly there was the sound of twigs breaking and leaves rustling. From out of the dense patch of trees just beyond the horsemen raced an animal, bearing down on her with alarming speed.

Miranda's attention wavered. The trance had been broken. Instead she focused on the giant beast headed toward her, its eyes fixed on hers.

Blue eyes.

It was Garth. Garth, shapeshifted into werewolf form.

For a fraction of a moment she was puzzled. And then she understood.

He was coming to save her. Somehow, he had known. He had sensed that something was wrong, that she was in trouble.

He had known her resolve would be weak.

She took only a moment to marvel at his ability to understand so much, so quickly, in such a mysterious manner.

In the next moment, all that was forgotten. She was suddenly facing the evil before her, understanding for the first time that its power could destroy not only her, but Garth as well.

Yet while she was overcome with fear, Garth appeared immune. She watched in astonishment as the werewolf crouched in front of the three horsemen, snarling and baring its teeth. Its blue eyes, edged in red, glowed in anger.

One of the horses, the one on the right, suddenly rose up on its hind legs, letting out a terrible whinny of fear. The werewolf stalked it, moving slowly, letting out a low, fearsome growl.

The horseman tried to steady the steed. The other horses grew more and more agitated. In vain their riders attempted to calm them.

And then, in one swift and sudden movement, the horse in the center jumped forward. The rider was confident, sitting erect, hardly moving at all. The werewolf backed off, its head kept low to the ground, its teeth still bared as it let out a threatening snarl. The two animals stood face to face, both frozen, both prepared to pounce.

And then a billow of foul-smelling smoke rose out from beneath the horse's hooves. Miranda glanced down, horrified, and saw that its feet were burning holes into the ground. When she looked back at the horse, she could see its eyes glowing, the same fiery red as burning embers.

Beneath the hood of the horseman's cloak, she could see a second pair of red eyes staring out.

Miranda could stand it no longer.

"Garth!" she cried, rushing over to the werewolf. "We have to get out of here!"

The wolf turned, its movements jerky.

"Please," she cried, her voice a near whisper. "Let's get out. Now!"

Their eyes met. In a fraction of a second, there was understanding.

The beast stood still while Miranda climbed

onto its back. It was so much larger than any ordinary wolf that she was able to ride it easily. She leaned forward, clasping her arms around its neck, digging her knees in tightly against the hard muscles of its side. Her head was next to the animal's neck, its golden fur a soft cushion against her face.

Away the beast raced. She was awed by its speed and its power. Effortlessly it traveled through the forest, leaving the three horsemen far behind.

She turned back once, afraid they would follow. Intuitively she knew they would not.

Still, as she and Garth sailed over a small stream and she realized it was over, she was shaking. Yes, they had gotten away. She was safe. But she could not deny the fact that she had tasted the evil power firsthand . . . and that the temptation had been so strong she had nearly surrendered.

CHAPTER 12

Miranda clung to the beast's neck as it crossed the rugged terrain with grace and ease, carrying her farther and farther through the forest and toward Cedar Crest. She kept her face buried in its soft fur, the warmth of its flesh protecting her from the bitter night. All around her, a sheeting rain was falling, the drops cold and hard, pelleting her with frightening force.

She'd expected to feel safe once they reached Cedar Crest. Yet as the beast slowed its pace and she peered out to see the stately mansion rising up with great dignity at the end of Winding Way, a feeling of dread came over her.

The house was different. It was surrounded by an aura, as if something were occupying it. Something cold. Something that didn't belong.

It's here, she thought. *It's followed us to Cedar Crest.*

She told herself she was mistaken.

Yet even as she tried desperately to convince herself, she understood why the power had come.

It had sensed her willingness to follow.

It knew. It had seen her weakness. The evil power understood that she had been attracted to it. That when she was forced to confront it, face to face, she'd found it irresistible, as so many had before her.

When they reached the house, the beast lay down and gently shrugged her off its powerful body. She lay in the grass, her eyes still fixed on the house, wrapped in the black of night yet somehow shrouded by an even greater darkness. Yes, she was certain; the evil presence was there. It hovered above, like a rain cloud. It was tentative, questioning.

"Are you with me?" it seemed to be asking. "You've experienced what's on the other side . . . and part of you was attracted to it. Will you let me draw you in again?"

Miranda shook her head hard, anxious to drive away the ominous feeling. When she heard someone come up behind her, she turned, relieved.

"Garth," she said, reaching out to him.

His face was drawn, clearly reflecting his exhaustion. His walk was that of someone completely drained: broad shoulders slumped, head down. He dragged his legs as if they were so heavy he could barely move them.

Even in the pale light of the crescent moon, she could see that telltale signs of the shape-shifting still remained. His arms seemed oddly long, his chest more massive than usual.

Yet it was his eyes that struck her most. She saw in them a wildness that she had never seen when he was in human form. It was the look of an animal. Alert. Fearful. On guard.

The moment she reached up and touched his hand, that look vanished. Suddenly he was Garth again—*her* Garth, the one she loved. It was over.

"Thank goodness you're safe." He curled up on the grass beside her, taking her in his arms. "I've never been so frightened in my life, Miranda. When I saw you standing before them . . ."

"I was afraid, too." She buried her face in his shoulder. "Hold me."

She clasped him tightly, relieved not to look him in the eye. She was unwilling to admit that what frightened her most was that single step she had taken.

"Who were they?"

He shook his head. "I don't know. I do know they've got something to do with the evil power that controls me." He hesitated. "They're after you, Miranda," he said, a catch in his throat.

"Yes," she said simply.

Suddenly he buried his face in her neck. "Oh, Miranda! This is the one thing I've feared most! That if you ever found out about me, that if my secret came out, they'd come after you."

"We'll fight it," she whispered hoarsely. "Together. And we'll win."

She only wished that, in her heart, she felt as certain as she sounded.

They stood at the French doors in the ballroom, looking out at the cold, hostile night. The rain beat down furiously, pounding against the glass as if demanding to be let in. Here inside Cedar Crest, it was warm and dry. Even so, Miranda found little comfort in this place of supposed refuge.

"We have to find out more," Miranda said, her eyes fixed on the silvery slivers of water streaking through the darkness. "We know so little. How can we fight something we don't understand?"

"Yes," Garth agreed. Putting his arm around her waist and drawing her closer, he let out a deep sigh. "But where do we begin?"

"We begin right here."

"I don't know what you mean."

"We begin in Overlook." She raised her face to his. "Don't you see, Garth? Everything is rooted right here. I'm not saying I understand how or why, but there are so many signs."

He thought for a moment, then nodded. "You're right." Looking around, he added, "There's Cedar Crest, of course. It's our most obvious link to the past—and to the curse that's plagued my family for generations."

"Yes. Your family's roots are here in town. Your grandfather lived here. His grandfather before him may have lived in Overlook, as well."

"I know he lived somewhere along the coast."

Miranda looked off into the distance, once again staring out into the night. "Devil's End," she said simply.

"What?"

"Have you ever wondered how Devil's End got its name?"

Garth shook his head in confusion. "I don't what you're talking about. What's Devil's End?"

"Devil's End is what the people around here call one particular section of the beach. Down at the bottom of the cliffs, right below Overlook. It's the most treacherous part. It was given that nickname back when the people around here lived almost exclusively off the sea. The rocks are so sharp that anybody or anything that crashed against them wouldn't stand a chance. Still, I've always wondered how it got that particular name. Now I can't help thinking it might have had something to do with the Wolf Clan."

There was a long pause. Miranda was thinking hard. She was so frustrated by how little she knew. It was like a puzzle, a puzzle for which she had the pieces, but no idea how they all fit together.

One piece was Overlook itself. Its bizarre

totem pole that sometimes seemed to have a life
of its own—a life that could well be linked in
some way to the dangerous stretch of beach
nicknamed Devil's End.

A second piece was the Gautier family and its
history. She had so much to learn. With a little
digging, she suspected she could uncover some
of the family's mysterious past.

Then there was Garth himself, destined to
live with the terrible legacy of the family curse.
The curse that tortured him with visions—visions so horrible they made him tremble, so inexplicable that, instead of helping him put the
pieces of his family's past together, they only
confused him even further. The curse that made
him the constant prey of an evil power so great
and so mysterious that mere humans like them
could barely grasp its meaning. The curse that
transformed him into a werewolf, a beast so terrible that for hundreds of years it had worked its
way into the frightening legends of countries all
over the world.

For a moment, Miranda felt overwhelmed.
She lay her head against Garth's shoulder, seeking the comfort that came from being close to
him. There were too many pieces in this puzzle
she was struggling with, none of them appear-
ing to fit together. However desperately she
longed to help Garth, she could not imagine
sorting through all the bizarre happenings of

the past weeks and coming up not only with a true understanding, but also the means of breaking the curse that bound him.

Yet she had to. Whatever it was was growing—in power, in control, in influence. While once the werewolf had killed only animals, it now sought other prey. While once the evil power had been content to linger in the background, it was becoming a greater and greater presence, foisting horrible visions upon Garth, hovering above his home . . . causing him to shapeshift more frequently than in the past, when only the full moon had transformed him.

While once it focused on Garth, it was now after her.

There had to be an answer. There had to be a way out. . . .

Suddenly she remembered still one more piece of the puzzle: the lore of the Native American tribes who had lived here for generations. They, too, had inhabited this land, along with the Gautier family . . . along with the evil power.

All of a sudden Miranda understood what she had to do.

"Garth," she said, her voice calm yet filled with resolve, "I know where we have to start."

As Garth hurried down Winding Way Monday afternoon, the giant hood on his parka shielding his face from the rain that continued to beat down, he took little heed of what was around him. He kept his eyes on the pitted dirt road he was traveling, now turned to mud. It was slippery in spots, rocky in others. Passing through safely required all his concentration.

Yet as he turned a bend in the road, he suddenly got the distinct feeling he was being watched. He pulled away his hood just enough to peer out.

Ahead of him, in the woods, a slight motion caught his eye. He stopped in his tracks, instantly on the alert.

Something was hiding in there.

He stood still for a long time, waiting. Around him, the steady downpour of pelting rain drowned out all the noises of the forest. Even though he strained, he could make out no sound.

And then, another movement.

This time he caught a glimpse of a lone figure. He darted out from behind a tree, his eyes lighting on Garth's for only an instant.

The man from the theater.

"Let me help you," he had said.

His puzzling plea had sent an icy shiver down Garth's back.

"Wait!" Garth called out on impulse. Instinctively he took a step in the man's direction, meanwhile holding out his arm.

It was too late. Already the man had vanished, slipping between the trees, losing himself among the dense growth of the forest.

For a moment, Garth wondered if it had merely been another vision.

Yet he knew. It was real.

The man was watching him.

He was tempted to follow him, to try to track him in the woods. But Miranda was waiting for him. So instead he hurried on his way, his forehead furrowed.

The Overlook Public Library was nearly empty, Garth observed as he stepped inside. The fluorescent lighting made him blink; its brightness seemed unnatural after the near darkness outdoors. As he sat down at one of the large reading tables, he was struck by the stillness of the place. Today, he felt so isolated, as if everywhere he went there was no warmth, no friendliness.

When he saw Miranda rush in, that feeling vanished. He decided then not to burden her with his report of the strange man who was watching him, keeping himself concealed by the dense growth of the forest. For now, they had another, more important mission.

"Ready?" she asked breathlessly. Her cheeks were flushed, but it was not from eagerness. That, he knew by looking into her dark eyes, intense and filled with apprehension.

The two of them approached Ms. Wallace, the library's head clerk. She was perched on a stool at the front desk, sorting books and lining them up neatly on a metal cart.

"Excuse me," Miranda said boldly. "We'd like to see the library's museum."

Ms. Wallace looked startled. She peered at them both through her bifocals. "Really?"

Garth glanced over at Miranda, surprised. "Isn't it open?"

"Yes, it is. It's just that—well, certainly you may see it. Things are pretty quiet right now, so I'll take you down myself." She reached into her skirt pocket and jiggled a set of keys, as if making certain they were there.

Garth and Miranda followed her in silence. The museum was in the basement, at the end of a long hallway. Ms. Wallace struggled with the lock, then flipped on a switch.

It took Garth a few seconds to adjust to the flickering yellowish fluorescent light. He walked into the center of the small, windowless room, his footsteps silenced by the thick gray carpeting. Glancing around, he was instantly intrigued.

The exhibit was more extensive than he'd expected. Glass display cases were lined up along all four walls. In them were various artifacts, pieces of the history of the Native Americans who had not long before been the sole inhabitants of Overlook. Arrowheads, mostly, but also pottery, wood carvings, and paintings on dried animal skins.

In one tall case there was an impressive display of beadwork, necklaces and headbands with intricate designs in a rainbow of colors. Alongside it was a long wooden table; on it, pieces of earthenware pottery were carefully arranged. Hung on the back wall was the mounted head of a bear, its glass eyes staring at the intruders coldly.

It was all magnificent, Garth thought. But what caught his attention most was a wolfskin, hanging inside the largest display case of them all.

It was huge, hanging from metal hooks that showed off its thick fur to its fullest. Its massive head was intact. The fierce expression made it look as if it were still alive: the pale eyes bright and intelligent, the jaw pulled back into a snarl, the sharp white teeth gleaming.

Garth was tempted to study it, but he was aware of Ms. Wallace's eyes upon him and Miranda as they circulated. So he pretended to focus instead on the cardboard boxes stacked up in one corner, looking extremely out of place in this otherwise meticulously kept room.

"You'll have to pardon those." Ms. Wallace leaned forward and wiped an imaginary bit of dust off the top of one of the glass display cases. "We're about to start packing everything away."

"Packing it away?" Garth was horrifed. "For good?"

The library clerk shrugged. "Truth is, hardly anybody ever comes down here. Oh, sure, we get a few school trips every year. Elementary-level kids, mostly. But I don't know that they get very much out of it.

"Besides, we need the space. We're planning on turning this into a computer center. Nothing fancy, mind you, but it's a start." With a sigh, she added, "Got to keep up with the times."

"Well, then, I'm glad we came," said Miranda.

"Feel free to take your time and look around. I'll be upstairs if you have any questions—"

"I have one already." Garth took a step toward the wolfskin enclosed in the glass case. "What exactly is this?"

"A wolfskin."

"But what's its significance?"

Ms. Wallace frowned, meanwhile heading over to where Garth was standing. "Mr. Trembley, the research librarian who worked here for decades before he retired a few years ago, did tell me a bit about these exhibits back when I first started working here. Let's see if I remember this correctly. I believe this was used in an old tribal ritual. . . ." She paused, glancing at the white card posted on the outside of the case. "Oh, that's right. The Native Americans used this in a ceremony in which they supposedly shifted into animal form."

Cautiously Garth glanced at Miranda. He saw that the startled expression on her face echoed what he was feeling. His heart was beating so hard he was afraid Ms. Wallace would hear it.

"I seem to recall something about herbs, as well." Ms. Wallace crouched down in front of the glass case in the corner.

Garth peered over her shoulder. Lined up on the bottom shelf, he saw rows of odd-looking dried herbs, twisted brown clumps tied together with string.

"Here we go," Ms. Wallace went on. "It's all explained right here, on these white cards in the case. Back in the old days, these herbs were an important part of a revered ritual. If someone wanted to change into an animal—let's say a wolf—he'd make a special concoction out of these herbs and smear it all over his body. Then he'd put the wolfskin over his body and draw two concentric circles on the ground."

She grimaced at the large display case. "Hmmm. Wonder if this was ever used for something like that."

She went back to her reading. "My goodness! Just listen to the names of some of these ingredients in that concoction! Hemlock, poplar leaves, bats' blood, sweet flag, mandrake . . ."

Ms. Wallace glanced up, casting Garth a bright smile. "Isn't that quaint?"

He simply nodded.

"I just love these colorful bits of folklore. They're primitive, but so charming. I've always meant to put some time in, learning more about them. . . .

"Now, all this is fascinating, but if you'll excuse me, I'd better get back to the front desk. I've already been away too long."

"Just one more question. What's that herb, over there?" Garth pointed to one that was set off from the others. There was a large clump of it, much more than the other clusters on display. It was also dried, with withered yellow flowers.

"That one is called monkshood. Its Latin name is *Aconitum lycoctonum.*" Ms. Wallace peered more closely at the white card. "Hmmm. It says here it's also called wolfsbane."

"Wolfsbane?" Miranda's voice was nearly a whisper.

This time Garth didn't dare look at her. "What was it used for?"

"According to what I remember," Ms. Wallace said, "the Native Americans believed it warded off evil."

CHAPTER
13

Back at Cedar Crest, Ms. Wallace's words continued to haunt Miranda. She was curled up on a velvet couch in the mansion's small library, its walls of wooden bookshelves lined with leather-bound volumes. She stared out the window, thoughtful as she gazed at the beauty of the forest. How splendid the rich colors were: the intense greens and warm browns running together in the rain like watercolor paints. The textures, too, were captivating: the softness of the moss, the spiky needles of the evergreens, the contrasting roughness of the trees' bark and the rocky terrain.

She had grown to love it here. The more time she spent in the lush gardens and in the elegant rooms, the more she came to think of it as her true home. She belonged at Cedar Crest. It had become as much a part of her as Garth.

She opened one of the windows, the fine

rain cold against her hand. The smell that wafted through was intoxicating. Greedily she inhaled the pungent scent of the cedars, the damp fragrant earth, the vibrant autumn air, newly cleansed by the downpour.

Suddenly Miranda found the lure of the forest irresistible. It was as if she'd become something else . . . a creature connected with the rest of nature in some fundamental way. A peculiar thought flitted into her mind: that the forest was a part of her.

"Garth?" Her eyes remained fixed on the view from the window.

"Yes?" He came over to her, resting his hands gently on her shoulders and bending down to plant light kisses on her neck.

"There's something I want to ask you."

"Anything."

She hesitated. "It's something you might not like."

"Miranda," he replied, "I'll give you whatever you want. You must know I could never say no to you."

Miranda stood up, whirling around so that she was facing him. Looking steadfastly into his eyes, she said, "Take me with you."

A look of confusion crossed his face. "I—I don't understand."

"I want to shapeshift."

He gasped.

"Take me on a hunt, Garth. You must. I want to run beneath the full moon. I want to feel the strength, the power, the *freedom* of being transformed into an animal. I want . . . I want to experience being a werewolf."

His expression darkened. "No, Miranda! You don't know what you're asking!"

"Yes, I do." She gripped his arms with tense hands. "I want to feel what you feel. I want to know what you know. Garth, I want to be what you are!"

He broke away from her grasp, burying his face in his hands. "No, Miranda. Anything but this."

"You must, Garth. You must help me."

"Miranda." He stood before her, his arms hanging limp at his sides, his eyes pleading. "You've got to forget this crazy idea. It's dangerous. Surely you must realize that! Could it really be possible that even after all that's happened, even after all you and I have gone through, you still don't understand . . . ?"

"I think I do," she interrupted. Her gaze was still fixed on his face. "I've gone head to head with the evil power, remember?"

"Yes." He cast her a rueful look. "And you didn't fare too well, either."

She winced. "I got away, Garth."

He acted as if he hadn't heard. "Besides, that was different," he insisted.

He turned and began pacing. "You were on the outside then. You're talking about changing into a werewolf. About crossing over to the other side. Miranda, how could you think for a moment I would ever help you go through the process that has made my entire life a living hell?"

"You have to," Miranda said simply.

"Why? Miranda, I don't understand."

Her tone was quiet but filled with certainty. "Because it's the only way I can help you fight."

He looked stunned, as if he'd just been struck across the face. Miranda rushed over to him, grabbing onto his arm.

"Don't you see, Garth?" she cried, giving in to the flood of emotions that up until this moment she'd been struggling to keep under control. "I have to experience the change. I have to become a werewolf. It's the only way I'll ever be able to truly understand the evil presence."

He clamped his eyes shut. Yet she never took her eyes off him. She was determined.

When he finally opened his eyes, the look on his face was one of torment. "Oh, Miranda. For so long I've tried to protect you from this evil. To keep it from you."

"Don't you see, Garth? I have to know. I have to know everything about it." Encircling him with her arms, she rested her head against his shoulder. "I have to know everything about *you*."

"There must be some other way—"

"There's no other way."

"How can you be sure?"

"Trust me, Garth," she said. "I'm sure."

His clasp was firm as he held her against him for a long time, saying nothing. She could hear his heart pounding violently.

"Wouldn't you be frightened?" he asked.

"You'd be there with me."

She raised her face so she could look into his eyes. She saw they were clouded with concern.

"If you were there," she told him, "I wouldn't be afraid at all."

There was a long, heavy pause. It was Miranda who broke it.

"Say yes. Say you'll help me."

"All right." His tone was one of defeat. "I will."

She simply nodded, nestling her head more closely against his chest.

Garth crouched beside a low shelf of books, holding his breath. He wanted to be completely certain he was alone before coming out of his hiding place.

The Overlook Public Library was eerily silent late on a Wednesday afternoon, the only sound the low hum of the heating system. Rather than the glaring fluorescent lights that usually lit up the main reading room, now only a few dim auxiliary lights banished the darkness. They cast long, oddly shaped shadows and created empty black spaces like the gaping mouths of caves.

Getting locked into the library after hours had been easier than he'd imagined. Ms. Wallace was in a hurry to get out, glancing over her shoulder at the clock every minute or so as she finished up her last-minute tasks before closing. Not once did she look over in his direction. He'd watched from behind a tall shelf in the reference section, keeping still, lying in wait. At two minutes after six, the clerk took a set of keys out of her skirt pocket and placed them in the top drawer of the desk behind the counter. Then she grabbed her coat and purse and hurried out the back door.

Now it was ten after. He'd stayed hidden in case she came back, but the empty room remained undisturbed. Suddenly it was time to spring into action. He knew he didn't have much time, since at some point during the evening a cleaning person was bound to be coming in.

He'd been so involved in carrying out his mission that it wasn't until he stood up that he remembered his true feelings about what he was about to do. He was still doubtful about Miranda's request that he help her change into a werewolf. His internal debate continued to rage even as he walked stealthily across the heavy carpeting after looking around one more time.

Part of him knew she was right. The evil

force had singled her out. It was pursuing her. She needed to understand it in order to fight.

Yet the question of whether or not she had the strength to combat it continued to haunt him. He had been powerless in its ruthless grasp; was she destined to suffer the same fate?

Perhaps, in the end, no one could resist.

She was afraid; he knew her well enough to be able to see through her brave front. Yet even stronger than her fear was her determination to help him fight, to find a way to banish the curse.

And so he remained uncertain. For years he had fought the power. Denounced it. Hated it. Above all, despised himself for what it made him.

And now he was going to help Miranda, the person in his life who meant more to him than anyone or anything else, to know that horror for herself. To watch her body transform. To know what it is to run exclusively on instinct. To see brought to the surface the animal nature that lurks inside every human being, yet which few are ever forced to confront head-on.

And above all, to be driven by the evil power.

Yet he had promised. It was too late to go back on his word.

Garth's palms were wet as he checked furtively around the library, knowing no one was around but still afraid that, somehow, someone had guessed what he was up to. The building was quiet. Even so, he kept glancing over his shoulder as he strode behind the counter, took the keys from the drawer, and slipped them into his pants pocket.

He was frightened. And the fact that he was about to steal from the library's museum was only a small part of it.

Downstairs, the long corridor edged with windowless rooms was forbidding. Long shadows crisscrossed the walls and floors. He walked slowly, every sound magnified a hundredfold. The pounding in his temples was a counterpoint to his short, quick breaths.

When he reached the end of the hallway, he hesitated outside the door.

It's not too late to go back. . . .

He shook his head, stubbornly ignoring the apprehensions that persisted in plaguing him. He unlocked the door, then slowly pushed it open. Darkness awaited him on the other side, empty black spaces that only gradually formed into glass display cases and tables as his eyes adjusted to the dim light.

He flipped on the switch, expecting that bathing the room in bright fluorescence would banish at least some of his uneasiness. The light flickered on, casting the room in its artificial brightness. Then, within a few moments, it went out.

Garth stood frozen to the spot, cloaked in

darkness, trying to digest what had just happened.

And then he understood. The fluorescent bulb had burned out; that was all it was.

Or was it?

He remained still, all his senses on full alert. He sniffed the air and pricked up his ears, meanwhile straining to see through the darkness. He was waiting for a sign that the evil power was present.

There was none.

He was disoriented for only a few seconds. He had come on a mission, and he had every intention of carrying it out. He went back upstairs, where the lights were still working. After scrounging around behind the counter a second time, he finally found what he needed. This time, when he went back down to the museum room, he was armed with a flashlight.

As he stood in the doorway and flicked it on, its dim light cast strange shadows throughout the room. He jumped at what he thought was someone leaping out at him. With a pounding heart he realized it was simply the tall case containing samples of Native American beadwork. The stuffed bear head glowered at him, looking particularly menacing with its glass eyes reflecting the light and its white teeth glowing.

For the first time since he'd come into the library this evening, he was tempted to give up.

He longed to turn and run. But he reminded himself he was doing this for Miranda as much as for himself. He remembered the pleading look in her eyes. The image of the three dark horsemen, standing before her, was burned into his brain.

And he recalled the urgency in her tone.

"It's the only way I can help you fight," she'd insisted.

She was right, he knew. The only way they could do it was together.

He found a small earthenware pot and used it to prop up the flashlight. Now his hands were free. They were trembling, he realized, staring at them, palms up in front of his face, as if they were odd, foreign objects. And they were damp, covered in sweat.

His whole body was bathed in perspiration.

Go back, the small, persistent voice inside his head warned once again. *It's not too late. Go back!*

He knew he would not.

Instead he reached into his pocket and stepped toward the display case in which the wolf-skin was housed. The small silver key, on the ring with all the other keys, fit easily inside the lock. He opened the glass door, then hesitated.

Go back!

Slowly, uncertainly, he reached for the giant pelt. As his fingers brushed against the soft fur, he paused, expecting to feel something, some power.

He felt nothing.

With the same cautious movements, he gripped the fur at the shoulder. As he did, he took care not to look at the animal's head, with its jaw frozen into a terrifying grimace. Carefully he lifted it off the metal hooks that held it in position.

It was surprisingly heavy. The head was immense, much larger than a human head. And the hide was huge, once the skin of an animal weighing one hundred eighty pounds and measuring more than six feet in length when it stood on all fours. The gray fur was thick and lustrous, a pale shade of gray flecked in spots with white. He had to strain to lift it.

Still he felt nothing. The thing he held in his hands was the pelt of a dead animal. Nothing more.

Yet he found it intriguing, much more so than any other object in the room. He was drawn to it.

He suddenly yearned to fling it over his back, to wear it like a cloak.

Just as Miranda would wear it when it was time for her to shapeshift. . . .

Go back!

He tried to ignore the voice. Yet he hesitated for only a moment. Already it seemed far, far away, its urgency lost on him. And then, in one fluid gesture, he draped the wolfskin over his back, the animal's shoulders aligned with his shoulders, its back superimposed over his back, its gigantic head resting heavily atop his own.

It was then that he felt the presence.

Almost immediately the air in the room changed. It became stifling, thick with a foul odor. The walls pulsated. Up from the floor rose a thunderous pounding: the hideous overamplified beating of a heart.

He no longer had any awareness of where he was. He knew only the all-encompassing yearning, a sensation that by now was familiar.

The longing to kill.

His bestial instincts urged him to flee the confining space, to escape, to roam the forest. . . .

And then the room vanished. The beast was racing through the woods. Its movements were confident, its determination strong.

It knew that tonight it would kill . . . again and again and again.

It was tireless as it raced through the forest, its senses powerful, its skill at locating its terrified victims at an apex. The beast's ability to hunt had never been sharper. Over and over again it chose its prey—a squirrel, a rabbit, a beaver—then zeroed in and pounced.

Twenty, thirty, forty animals. One by one he claimed his victims.

Yet the beast felt no hunger.

It was not for itself that it killed. Tonight the beast operated like a machine. Dispassionate.

Efficient. Going through the process with swift yet mechanical movements.

It didn't feed. Instead, after each attack it picked up its victim in its slackened jaws and carried it to one particular spot in the forest. As the pile grew, it experienced something vaguely like pleasure.

Still, there was no understanding. Only the certainty that this was what it must do to survive.

It became aware of the presence of other creatures—not animals, humans. Far away, in the distance, it spotted a small building, made from rough-hewn logs. Black smoke rose out of a brick chimney.

Somewhere in the area, there were guns; the beast's sensitive nose easily picked up the acrid odor of gunpowder. There were many dead animals, as well, their skins stripped away from their lifeless bodies.

At the moment, the beast did not understand any of it. What it did know was that it was part of it. That somehow this stockpiling of animal skins had something to do with its own repeated killings.

Kill more.

It longed to race among the tall trees of the forest, hunting with a skill none of the humans could ever match, winning the respect and admiration of those whose abilities as hunters could never come even close to his.

Knowing their love of killing—their _need_ to kill—could never match that of the werewolf. . . .

"_No!_"

He didn't know where the voice came from. Nor did he recognize the source of the sudden surge of strength that caused him to act. All he knew was that he suddenly found himself standing in the middle of the museum, his heart pounding, his body dripping with perspiration, his mind racing. Behind him, on the floor in a heap, lay the fur.

The room was quiet. He was alone.

Gingerly he picked up the animal skin. Once again, he felt nothing. Only the most immediate sensations: the softness of the fur, the warmth from his own body.

He understood immediately that it had all been nothing more than yet another vision.

None of it had been real.

He was tempted to flee. But he calmed himself, reminding himself of the mission he was determined to carry out.

He steadied his trembling hands enough to unlock a second glass display case. From the collection of herbs, each identified on neat, handwritten cards, he made his choices, knowing instinctively which he would need.

He gathered up the wolfskin, bracing himself against its weight, then stole out of the library, his movements as furtive and fast as those of an animal.

CHAPTER
14

The moon was a mere sliver, a pale crescent tucked into one corner of the sky. The stars shone weakly, little more than dim flecks against a shroud of black.

Miranda stood in the ballroom, gazing out through the French doors. How different everything looked tonight. How forbidding . . . yet at the same time how enticing.

It was a peculiar feeling, knowing she was about to become a part of the night.

"Are you sure?" Garth came up behind her and wrapped his arms lightly around her waist.

"Yes. I'm sure."

"It's not too late to change your mind."

It is too late, she was thinking. *The evil power has already done too much damage—to you, to us—to turn back now. We have to fight it. And in order to fight it, I have to understand it.*

But she didn't say any of those things. Instead she turned to face him, encircling his neck with her arms and looking into his blue eyes. Just as she'd hoped, in those eyes she found the strength she needed.

"Is it time?"

Garth's gaze traveled to the window. She studied his face. His forehead was creased in concentration. But it was the tension around his mouth that conveyed his concern. He'd never liked the idea of bringing her along with him on a hunt, of helping her to experience shapeshifting firsthand. She was aware of his fears, and she yearned to sooth him.

But tonight those fears created a distance between them. She couldn't reach him the way she usually could. As he stood looking out at the night, she could see he was cut off from her, too absorbed in his own apprehensions to reach out to her—or to allow her to reach out to him.

And then he turned to her. His voice was hoarse as he gripped her tightly and said, "Let's go."

He retrieved the giant wolfskin from the corner of the ballroom, where it lay in a heap. After throwing a jacket over her shoulders, Miranda gathered up the wooden bowl containing the pungent concoction of herbs he'd mixed up earlier.

The biting November air stung her cheeks as

she stepped outside. Wordlessly she followed Garth through the garden. The two of them climbed over a crumbled section of the wall, into the forest that surrounded Cedar Crest.

They walked until they came to a clearing. Side by side they stood, both silent, both tense. Finally she glanced down at the bowl in her arms.

"What's this for?" she asked in a pinched voice.

"When the time is right, you'll need to rub it over your body."

"What's in it?"

"It doesn't matter."

"I want to know," she insisted. "Please, Garth."

"I'm sorry." Instantly his voice softened. "It's just that . . . I keep trying to protect you, Miranda."

"The best way I can protect myself," she told him, "is to know everything. *Everything.*"

"All right." He took a deep breath. "It's a mixture of ingredients made from plants. Those herbs on display in the library, mostly."

"Which herbs, Garth?"

"Wolfsbane is one of them. There are others, as well: deadly nightshade, sweet flag, hemlock, and mandrake. I also put in poplar leaves and soot."

She swallowed hard. "How did you know what to use?"

His face was expressionless. "I just knew." He held out the fur. "Let's start, Miranda."

She was suddenly awed by the momentousness of what they were about to do. Her heart was pounding wildly. She felt dizzy and out of control. It was like being in a state of freefall.

"What do I have to do?"

"There are three steps." Garth's tone was even and controlled. "First, smear the herb potion all over your body."

Miranda gave a curt nod of her head, then dropped her jacket to the ground. Glancing at Garth, she noticed him averting his eyes. Quickly she slipped off the rest of her clothes. The night air was cool against her skin. She shivered as she stuck her fingers into the bowl, scooping up some of the odd-smelling mixture. It was gritty and cool, not at all pleasant. But she refused to let herself think about it. Instead she set to work. Bracing herself against the strange sensation, she began covering her arms, her neck, and her face with the brown concoction. It was repulsive at first. But before long her skin began to tingle. It was an odd feeling; her flesh actually seemed to be absorbing the potion.

The mixture affected her mind, as well. Her thoughts were growing clouded. She was quickly losing her grip on what was happening around her.

Her instinctive reaction over the loss of control she was experiencing was panic.

"Garth," she said breathlessly, "I feel strange."

She closed her eyes, then forced them open. Even through her haze she could see that the look on his face was one of concern.

"Miranda!" He grasped her shoulders. "It's not too late to go back."

"No," she insisted. "I want to go forward."

He hesitated. Then he lifted the heavy wolf-skin up onto her shoulders. "This is the second step."

She leaned forward as he spread it out across her back. The animal fur was heavy, much more so than she'd expected. She nearly fell when he placed the wolf's massive head atop her own.

"Are you sure you can manage?" he asked.

"Yes. I have to." The sound of her own voice startled her. It sounded so far away.

The forest was swirling around her, the browns and greens running into one another in an ever-changing pattern. She was having trouble focusing on what was happening. And so she simply gave in to it, putting herself in Garth's hands.

"Stand over here." With a stick, Garth drew two concentric circles in the dirt. The one in the middle was just large enough for her to fit into.

"This is the third step," he said. "Once you stand inside, the process is complete."

Struggling under the weight of the wolfskin, Miranda moved toward the circles. She felt she was in a dream; everything seemed real, yet somewhere in the back of her mind she kept thinking none of this could actually be happening.

And then she stepped into the circle.

Instantly a ring of fire sprang up around her. Orange flames leaped upward, illuminating the clearing with their flickering light. Oddly shaped shadows jumped out from behind trees, from under bushes, their ghoulish forms shifting and reshaping. A low rhythmic rumble, like the pounding of drums, rose up from the bowels of the earth. High-pitched noises shot out of the forest, the deafening shrieks of creatures that were neither animal nor human.

Miranda threw back her head, letting a groan escape her lips. She could feel the heat of the fire burning her ankles, the black curls of smoke doing an ominous dance around her. Suddenly it was overwhelming: the heat, the weight of the wolfskin, the strange sounds rising out of the forest and out of the ground. She felt faint. She longed to clamp her hands over her ears, to shut her eyes tight against the barrage of noise and heat and light. A scream was rising from deep inside, a scream of fear, of desperation, of supplication. . . .

And then, suddenly, she felt a surge of power. The wolfskin was no longer heavy. The fire was no longer hot.

The shrieking sounds from the forest no longer frightened her.

Instead, she felt at one with her surroundings. A part of the forest in a way she had never been before.

Slowly the dazed feeling was slipping away. She gradually became aware that everything looked different. The trees were taller, the stars farther away. All her senses were bizarrely acute. She could smell things she'd never smelled before. The richness of the soil. The scent of an animal scampering through the woods. She could hear things she'd never heard before. And she could see for miles.

Miranda glanced down. Her own body had vanished. In its place was one she didn't recognize.

She had been transformed into an animal.

Werewolf.

It was done. The change had taken place.

She marveled at her new form. Fascinated, she studied her long limbs, covered in wiry black fur. She could feel the strength of her muscles, the mass of her chest and neck. Her head was different, as well; her jaw was long and powerful, her ears pointed, her teeth sharp.

She looked to the side. A giant animal stood next to her, its posture proud and erect, its thick golden fur glistening, its blue eyes piercing into hers.

Garth. He, too, had been transformed. She was intensely aware of the heat emanating from his body, his musky smell, the sound of him panting.

Now the two of them were free to run. To roam the forests. To hunt.

To connect, to be together in a way they never had before.

It was exhilarating. The anticipation of what was to come made it difficult for Miranda to breathe. Every nerve was alive, prickling with expectation.

And then there was no more reason. No more logic. No more thought of resisting.

All that was left was Garth . . . and the night.

They ran side by side, stride matching stride, their movements rhythmic. They leaped over swampy bogs and craggy rocks, chests heaving and muscles taut, their breaths coming quick and hard. The two animals moved swiftly and gracefully, together conquering the night.

Never before had Miranda known such exhilaration. Her instincts took over, allowing her to experience being in the forest in a way she never had before. How magnificent it felt to run so fast! To see so far, to hear so much . . .

Even stronger than her heightened senses and her physical power, however, was her sense of herself as an animal. She felt a part of nature, connected to all the other living creatures. The soft, damp earth beneath her; the clear, icy air;

the lush growth of fragrant evergreens: she was linked to it all.

Even as she raced through the forest with Garth at her side, Miranda was still aware of who she really was. She was watching herself, marveling at the changes her body was going through, dazzled by the onslaught of sensations.

She was aware of Garth in a new way, as well. The warmth of his body as he ran beside her, his impressive strength and speed, his scent . . . the feeling that the two of them were joined, coconspirators in an exciting adventure. She felt close to him. In tune with him. Part of him.

Suddenly something caught her attention. She slowed her pace, noticing that Garth was doing the same. They'd picked up the same scent.

She didn't know what it was. It was not a pleasant odor, yet it was nevertheless oddly enticing. Her mouth grew moist, her muscles tensed.

A new feeling surfaced, one she'd never experienced before.

It was strong. Overwhelming, in fact. The part of her that remained human puzzled over what it could possibly be.

And then she knew. It was the urge to hunt. To feed.

To kill.

Suddenly Garth broke into a run. She could sense his determination. Growing excited, she raced after him, amazed at how easily she kept the pace. Her heartbeat quickened, her senses sharpened. Adrenaline shot through her veins, infusing her with almost supernatural strength.

And then she saw it. Standing in a small clearing, feeding on tall grasses . . . an elk, its body sleek and muscular, its stance proud, its movements graceful. Atop its head was a massive pair of antlers.

The wolves moved toward it soundlessly. For a long time they lay in wait, concealed by bushes, watching the giant animal feed. Miranda followed Garth's lead, copying his movements. At the same time her own instincts were strong.

All of a sudden, the moment was right. Moving together, acting as one, Garth and Miranda sprang forward, bounding into the clearing.

For a fraction of a second, she saw the terror in the elk's eyes.

And then she knew nothing but the power of her need. She and Garth pounced upon the huge animal. It tried to flee, turning quickly but losing its balance as its hooves slipped against the muddy soil.

She was acting completely on instinct. There was no longer any contact with her human side, nothing to hold her back. She knew only the thrill of the hunt. The joy of giving in to her bestial instincts.

The ecstasy that could only come from total release.

* * *

Miranda lay on the ground in front of Cedar Crest, her breaths so heavy they were nearly gasps. Her muscles ached from exhaustion and her skin was damp.

The morning sun barely peeked over the horizon. All around her, the new day was being born. Eagerly she drank it in. The sweet fragrance of the grass, sprinkled with dew. The rich smell of the moist soil. The colors of the sky, streaks of orange and pink and gold against dark blue lightening to pale aqua.

In her mind she relived the long night she had just spent. Roaming the forest, hunting, experiencing a freedom unlike anything she had ever known before. And through it all, Garth had been at her side.

She realized then that she was not alone.

"Garth?" She turned and saw him lying in the grass beside her.

"I'm here, Miranda." He took her hand, interlacing his fingers with hers.

For a long time the two of them lay side by side in silence. And then Garth asked, "Are you all right?"

She paused before replying. "It was wonderful."

Feeling him stiffen beside her, Miranda braced herself for the barrage of protests she knew would follow.

Yet instead of launching into an angry tirade, he shook his head tiredly. "No, Miranda," he said, his voice filled with defeat.

His words barely touched her. The reason Miranda had first decided to embark on this adventure had been so she could learn about the power, to understand the mysterious force she had pledged to fight. And now, after having experienced shapeshifting herself, she did understand.

She'd realized that its strength was rooted only partly in the evil force. Even more important was the willingness of the human spirit to succumb to its lure.

CHAPTER
15

Walking home through the emerging dawn, Miranda felt oddly energized. She hadn't slept the night before, yet she wasn't at all tired. Her senses were heightened, her experience of herself acute.

Her perception of the world was more intense than ever before. She reveled in the feeling of being in the midst of the forest, surrounded by the stark black trunks of trees, their twisted branches reaching out to her through the undulating coils of white morning mist.

Being in the forest suddenly felt brand-new.

Once she had been an outsider here in this moist, green world, someone allowed merely to visit, to observe, to sample what it meant to be part of it, but only for a short while.

Now Miranda belonged here.

She was connected with nature in a way she

never had been before. The plants and the animals, all the living things on earth . . . she was bound together with them, every one.

They were all interdependent, all part of the same glorious whole.

Walking home through the woods, she took her time, lingering to enjoy what only the day before she would not have even noticed. When she came across a patch of wild mushrooms, she relived the joy of inhaling their subtle scent with the sharp olfactory senses of an animal, throwing her head back and letting the sensation wash over her once again. Looking around the forest, she eagerly picked up on the variations in color. She understood the different shades of green in a new way, experiencing them for what they meant: the pale green of newer growth, the dark hues of more mature plant life. She noticed a symphony of new sounds: insects buzzing, dried leaves fluttering in the faintest breeze, twigs snapping off branches as squirrels scampered through the trees.

Even the animals seemed to sense the change she had undergone. Was it only her imagination, or did they really scurry away from her more quickly than before, as if they knew of the magnificent power she had only hours earlier possessed?

She passed through a clearing, stepping carefully over a muddy spot edging the small stream that curved through. It was a relief to pass through to the other side, finding herself surrounded by dense forest growth once again.

Suddenly she started. Ice-cold fingers, hard and wrinkled, grabbed hold of her arm.

Letting out a loud gasp, Miranda turned.

"Featherwoman!" she exclaimed. "You scared me. I thought I was alone."

"We are never alone in the forest," the old woman replied. "This, you already know."

Her leathery face was tensed into an earnest expression, her jet-black eyes piercing. Accusing. Their hardness made Miranda want to turn away. Yet she remained frozen to the spot.

"I can feel them." Featherwoman closed her eyes, lifting her face upward.

"What? What can you feel?"

"The narnauks. They are here."

Miranda could barely speak. "The good spirits?"

"The evil spirits." The Native American woman's eyes opened. "Listen to me, Miranda. They are rejoicing. I can hear their malevolent singing. I can feel the vibrations from their wicked dance."

Miranda took a step backward. "I—I don't know what you're talking about."

"They are celebrating."

Miranda could feel the color drain out of her face. And then the old woman reached for her, grabbing her by the shoulders.

"I know what you've done," she hissed. "I can see it in your eyes."

"No! You're wrong! I was only trying to—"

"Hear me, my child! What you are doing is dangerous. Don't you understand? This is what they want! This is what *it* wants!"

The old woman's words sent a chill down Miranda's spine.

"It?" she repeated slowly. "What is 'it'?"

"The Evil One. The darkest of them all." The woman's face was contorted into an expression of horror. "You are going too far."

All of a sudden Miranda buried her face in her hands. "I have to. I have no choice."

"There is always a choice."

"I must learn what it's all about. I need to know what it means!"

"You have crossed over to the other side," Featherwoman rasped. "Don't you understand there is no going back?"

"It came for me, Featherwoman! The three dark horsemen . . ."

"You could have resisted."

"I still can!" Miranda insisted. "I know I can!"

"Once you have passed over the line, the power has you in its grip. Soon it will be too strong to fight."

"I had to!" Miranda's voice was edged with hysteria. "It was our only hope."

"Beware, Miranda. I have seen the past. And

I know the future. There is trouble to come. You must be prepared—"

"Tell me!" she pleaded. "What's going to happen, Featherwoman?"

"Stay away, Miranda. The Evil One has set a trap . . . and already you are slipping into it."

"But it's what I chose!"

The old woman didn't seem to have heard. "You have strayed but once. Perhaps it is not yet too late; the Evil One grows more powerful over time. But heed my warning. Resist, Miranda. Fight it with your heart and your soul.

"Fight it now, before it has grabbed hold of you. Because once it does, it will never let go."

The encounter with Featherwoman left Miranda shaken. She was exhausted, she realized, as she let herself into the house and got ready for school. It was impossible for her to think clearly. She decided to put her agitation aside, to mull over Featherwoman's words of warning after she'd gotten through her day of classes.

The minute she got home from school, she headed for her bedroom—relieved that she didn't run into her mother—and immediately sank into a deep sleep. When she woke up, the sun was low in the sky. Miranda felt disoriented. It took her a long time to shake the dazed feeling that persisted, making her feel as if her mind had been coated with cobwebs. As she showered and put on fresh clothes, she tried to concentrate on what she was doing. Yet she kept going back, thinking about the night before, reliving the same feelings.

Standing in front of her mirror, she stared at her reflection for a long time, wondering if the different way she now felt showed on her face. All she could see was a glow on her skin and a clearness in her eyes. Other than that, she looked the same.

Realizing she was ravenous, she headed downstairs to the kitchen. It was filled with wonderful smells. A chicken was roasting in the oven, and a chocolate cake, freshly baked, sat on the counter.

"Mom?" she called, curious about the special preparations. Already her experience of the night before was fading into the background.

Mrs. Campbell was in the dining room, fussing with a bouquet of flowers in an elegant cut-glass vase. The table was set with a pastel flowered tablecloth, one of her mother's favorites. Arranged on it was the family's good china. There were three places set.

"Expecting company?" Miranda asked.

"In a way." Mrs. Campbell glanced up from the dried foliage she was arranging. "Your father."

"He's coming to dinner?"

She nodded. "We're really trying to see if we can find a way to talk to each other without our old conflicts getting in the way." Her cheeks were flushed as she added, "Every time we see each other, we seem to get along better and better."

Miranda tried to keep her hopefulness in check. "That's great, Mom."

"By the way, a letter came for you." Her mother's voice sounded odd. "I left it on the coffee table."

"Who's it from?" Miranda was already heading toward the living room.

"Oh, nobody important." Her mother paused. "Just the Limelight Theater Company."

A few moments later, Miranda let out a squeal.

"They've invited me to Portland for an audition!" She dashed back into the dining room, the letter in her hand. "Next Monday. That's only a few days away! I'll have to take off from school, too. Oh, Mom, please say I can go!"

Mrs. Campbell came over to her daughter and put her arms around her. "Of course you can go."

Miranda hugged her mother back. Over her shoulder she could see the flowers, the tablecloth, the fine china. There was even a pair of candles in silver candlestick holders.

Suddenly a thought that had been lurking at the back of her mind ever since she'd first skimmed the letter came into focus. The day of the audition, there was going to be a full moon.

"Miranda, can I talk to you for a minute?"

Miranda was coming out of the school cafeteria early Friday afternoon, chatting with Laura, when Bobby approached her. Nervously he pushed his dark brown hair out of his eyes.

Glancing at Laura, she asked, "Do you mind?"

"Of course not. I'll catch you later, Miranda."

Miranda and Bobby moved to the side of the corridor, standing in front of a bulletin board covered with student artwork. She looked at him expectantly.

"What is it?"

"I, uh, wanted to apologize for Amy."

"You don't have to, Bobby," she returned sincerely. "I know that, whatever Amy does, it has nothing to do with you."

"I'm glad you understand that." He lowered his eyes. "It's just that . . . well, it's important to me that you know I don't agree with her. In fact, I think it's pretty crummy the way she's been going around telling everybody she thinks Garth had something to do with those attacks. She and I have been arguing about it ever since she started up."

He paused before adding, "Now she's got this thing about Mark O'Neill's accident. As if it was anybody's fault but his that he was stupid enough to be lighting fires in the forest."

"I never thought you had anything to do with the things Amy's been saying," said Miranda. "But thank you. It means a lot to me that you're being so honest."

Bobby glanced at her, his cheeks flushed. "Well, uh, that's really all I had to say."

Miranda nodded. "Okay, then. I'll see you around."

"Right. See you."

He began walking away, then suddenly turned back. "Hey, Miranda?"

"Yes?"

"I was just wondering . . . do you ever think about how it used to be? With us, I mean. Back when things were still good."

"Of course I do," Miranda replied, her voice soft. "How about you?"

He stood perfectly still for a moment, his eyes burning into hers. "All the time."

CHAPTER
16

"Oh, Elinor, I'm so excited! I can't believe this is really happening . . . that I'm going to audition for a professional theater company!"

Miranda glanced at her friend, sitting beside her in the front seat of the car. It was her mother's, on loan for this special occasion. Elinor was leaning back comfortably in the passenger seat beside Miranda, the wide grin on her face making it clear she was really enjoying this chance to drive up to Portland for a two-day visit.

"You deserve it, Miranda. Besides, it's the director of the Limelight Theater Company who should be excited. He's the one who's about to have his socks knocked off!"

For the hundredth time since she'd gotten into the car two hours earlier, Miranda peered into the rearview mirror to check her appearance. She kept hoping she looked fresh, that there were no telltale signs that she'd barely slept a wink the night before.

She'd been too stirred up. This was the day she'd been waiting for ever since Robert Dolan had stopped by to invite her to audition for Portland's premier theater company. Now, finally, it was really happening. She and Elinor were driving up for two days—Miranda, to live out one of her lifetime dreams; Elinor, to provide moral support.

She'd been up at six, getting ready, reciting the lines in the scene she'd prepared for the audition as she blow-dried her hair. Yet what was at least as important, she knew, was being relaxed. If she didn't find a way of keeping her excitement in check, she'd never be able to give her best performance at the audition.

Despite her anticipation, despite all the preparations she'd made, feelings of ambivalence had continued to gnaw at her. She'd felt bad about leaving Garth—especially tonight. Yet he'd wanted her to go.

"This is important to you, Miranda. Of course I want you to go," he'd insisted, looking earnestly into her eyes as he clutched both her shoulders with his strong hands. "The last thing I'd ever do is stand in your way."

"But the full moon," she'd protested. "I thought we'd decided to fight this together."

He'd shaken his head. Smiling, he told her, "I'll be fine."

And so she'd done her best to put her concerns aside. She knew that, tonight, part of her would be with him. For now, that was the best she could offer.

As she drove north along the Oregon coast, Miranda reviewed everything Mr. Dolan had told her on the phone, just three days earlier. The audition was set up for eleven o'clock that morning. She'd be meeting with David Singer, the man chosen to direct Jean-Louis Boucher's experimental new play. He wanted her to do a scene from *Saint Joan*, whichever one she chose. In addition she'd be asked to do a cold reading, some lines from the script of the new play itself.

That was only part of it. She'd also be meeting other members of the troupe. It was important to fit in, to be able to interact with the other actors offstage as well as on.

Almost as if she were reading her mind, Elinor suddenly interjected, "You've got absolutely nothing to worry about, Miranda. You'll be great at your audition. And everybody in the theater company is going to love you."

Miranda glanced over at her friend, her face relaxing into a smile. "Thanks, Elinor. And thank you for coming with me today. It'd be much harder if I were doing this alone."

"Are you kidding?" Elinor cried. "This is the

most thrilling thing that's happened to me in weeks! Going to Portland, meeting actors, rubbing elbows with the theater crowd . . . what could possibly be more glamorous?" There was a twinkle in her eye as she added, "Besides, I'm getting to take a day and a half off from school . . . *and* get a head start on my Christmas shopping. Now, that's my idea of fun!"

Miranda laughed. Elinor was right; this *was* fun. The butterflies in her stomach aside, she had to admit it was a great feeling, taking to the road like this. While the November day was chilly, winter already very much a presence, the sun was brilliant and the sky was a soft shade of robin's-egg blue. Not a single cloud cluttered the horizon.

She felt wonderfully free, embarking on this trip. It was an adventure. Going into the city, living out one of her lifelong fantasies . . . and doing it with a good friend at her side. At that moment, the fears and conflicts that had been such a part of her life over the past few weeks were all but forgotten.

Miranda's eyes were wide as she drove into downtown Portland. She'd visited the city before, on school trips or with her parents, but this time was different. She was coming not as a sightseer, but with a special purpose. She was here to live out a dream she'd had ever since she was a little girl.

"There it is!" Elinor suddenly squealed. She was pointing straight ahead.

On the corner was the Limelight Theater. Miranda's heart was pounding as she studied the narrow, red brick building, a dignified structure three stories high. Its name was printed boldly on colorful banners flying overhead. In front, framing the main entrance, were large posters announcing the company's current productions.

"Wow!" Elinor cried. "It's fantastic! Oh, Miranda, I just know you're destined to be a part of all this."

Miranda cast her a rueful glance. "Not if I'm late for my audition. It's already quarter of eleven." She peered into the rearview mirror. "Do I look all right?"

"Relax, Miranda. You'll be fine." She pointed out the window. "There's even a parking space right over there. A good omen, I'd say!"

Miranda parked, then turned to face Elinor. "You're sure you'll be all right?"

"While you're auditioning, I'm going to be playing the role of tourist." Elinor gestured toward the sneakers she was wearing. "See? I'm even dressed for the part!"

After the girls exchanged a quick hug, Elinor left, calling a heartfelt, "Break a leg!" over her shoulder.

This is it, Miranda was thinking as she stood

outside the stately building, taking a few deep breaths and attempting to quiet her pounding heart. *This is really it.*

And then she pushed open the doors, passed through the lobby, and stepped into the theater.

It took a few seconds for her eyes to get used to the dim light inside. The walls and ceiling were painted black, and only a few houselights were on. Once she did adjust, she saw that it was a small space. There was no actual stage. Instead, seats rose up along three sides, creating an informal yet intimate atmosphere. Overhead, in a complicated grid pattern, were dozens, if not hundreds, of lights.

Miranda found she derived a sense of serenity from being here in this theater. It felt right. She had a feeling Elinor had been correct when she'd said she really did belong here.

She was so enthralled by the theater that she didn't realize at first that she wasn't alone. She started when she noticed a young man sitting in the first row, his head bent over what appeared to be a script. He had dark hair, worn a bit long, and was dressed in jeans and a faded blue shirt. Miranda was struck by how handsome he was; her first thought was that he had the look of a leading man.

He glanced at her, looking her up and down as if he were assessing her.

"You're early," he said.

"I'm sorry. I could come back later—"

"No, no. Not at all. Promptness is a virtue, especially in the theater."

He stood up then, his face finally softening into a smile. His eyes were green, Miranda noticed. And he was even better-looking up close.

"Are you David Singer?"

The young man snickered. "Me? No. I'm just a lowly actor."

Miranda laughed, too. But as she studied his face, she couldn't tell if he was teasing her or simply making conversation.

"To be more accurate, I'm a lowly actor who calls himself Jeff Jordan." He shrugged. "Not very original, but it was the best my parents could come up with."

"Hello, Jeff. I'm Miranda—"

"Miranda Campbell. The most astonishing Saint Joan the great state of Oregon has ever laid eyes on."

She was silent for a moment. There it was again, that feeling that he was mocking her. Or maybe it was just his way of being friendly.

"That's me," she replied.

"I'm going to be reading with you at your audition. That's how David likes to do it."

"Oh, are you trying out for the play too?"

"Me? No way. I'm already in the theater company, so my days of suffering the agony of auditions are over." Jeff grinned. "David is already convinced I'd make a great Commander. That's the male lead in _La Rose_. Yes, I've had a feeling this part was made for me ever since I first heard about it. Fortunately, it turns out that great minds think alike."

Miranda was trying to think up something appropriate to say when the door opened. In stepped a plump man, dressed in a white suit with a purple shirt. A turquoise scarf was draped around his neck. He carried a script in one hand; in the other was the largest cup of coffee she'd ever seen.

"Eleven o'clock," he groaned. "What a ridiculous hour of the morning to start one's day! I'm surprised it's not still dark out."

"This," Jeff announced, "is David Singer. Our most humble director."

"Director, yes. Humble, hardly." David Singer leaned forward and peered at Miranda. "I'd shake your hand, but as you can see I'm up to my elbows in caffeine."

"That's all right. I—"

"So you're Tyler's protégée." He, too, looked her up and down. "Well, I've always trusted his judgment. And he certainly had enough good things to say about you."

Miranda expected to feel herself blush. But she was beginning to understand that this was simply how theater people talked.

"Let's get down to business, shall we? You

know that old saying: idle hands are the devil's
. . . whatever." The director sat down in the
front row, then peered up at Miranda expectantly. "So, what little theatrical tidbit are you
going to be delighting us with this morning?"

"A scene from *Saint Joan.*"

"Ah, yes." David sighed. "Let's hear it for the
lady in red."

It took Miranda a few seconds to realize she
was expected simply to launch into her recita-
tion. No preparation, no background, no help
from anyone. And so she took a deep breath,
took a moment to focus her thoughts, and
began.

The excerpt she had chosen was an impas-
sioned speech made by Joan of Arc in which she
pleads for an army so she can help fight her
beloved homeland's worst enemy. At first Miranda was nervous. It was strange, standing in the
middle of a stage, surrounded on three sides by
rows of seats that were empty except for two lone
souls.

But her voice was even and strong. Hearing
the familiar words, delivered with confidence,
propelled her onward. Before long she was
caught up in the monologue, forgetting all
about the awkwardness of the situation. Instead,
she once again became the Maid of Orléans.

When she stopped, she was greeted by a long
silence. David Singer finally cleared his throat.

"Well, Tyler wasn't completely wrong. You're certainly chock-full of potential."

He turned to Jeff. "Do you agree?"

Miranda could feel her cheeks growing hot as she felt Jeff Jordan's admiring eyes upon her. For the first time since they met, he seemed to have nothing to say.

Miranda stood on the corner, directly in front of the Limelight Theater, feeling a mixture of relief and disappointment. The audition had been over so quickly. Even the brief reading she'd given with Jeff, a short scene she'd been barely given time to glance through beforehand, had gone by in a flash. Now came the hard part: waiting for David Singer's decision. It was early, barely eleven thirty, but she was hungry. She was on her own until one o'clock, when she was scheduled to meet Elinor. Her plans included getting something to eat. Miranda scanned the row of shops that stretched out before her, wondering which of the half-dozen restaurants to choose.

"Pasta Palace isn't bad," she suddenly heard a voice behind her say. "Of course, if you like Mexican food, you can't go wrong with Don Juan."

She glanced over her shoulder. "Are you a mind reader, Jeff?"

"Hey," he returned with a shrug. "I see somebody checking out the restaurants, the sun's high in the sky . . . put them all together, the signs spell 'lunch.' "

"I do like Mexican food—"

"Me, too. Let's go."

Miranda hadn't anticipated having a lunch date, especially with Jeff Jordan. He was certainly a good actor; that much, he'd proven during the reading. But she had yet to make up her mind about him.

Still, there was no reason not to have lunch with him. She followed his lead into a small Mexican café, a bustling place painted in bright shades of yellow and orange and decorated with piñatas and colorful paper flowers.

"So tell me, Miranda," he said after they'd been seated at a small table next to the window. "How long have you had the acting bug?"

Miranda smiled. "For as long as I can remember, I've wanted to do something special. Acting was just one possibility. I longed to be a great writer or a scientist or an artist . . . maybe even a philosopher. I've always dreamed of distinguishing myself in some way, of accomplishing something that made me special. Something nobody else could do."

She laughed, suddenly self-conscious. "All this must sound rather silly to you."

"No, not at all." Jeff gazed at her for what felt like a very long time, meanwhile circling the rim of his water glass with his finger. "As a matter of fact, I'm finding all this quite charming."

Miranda was relieved that their waiter chose that moment to bring their menus.

"How about you?" she asked conversationally as she scanned the listings. "How did you end up with the Limelight Theater Company?"

Jeff sighed. "It's been a long haul for me. I started acting when I was a kid. Four years old, in fact. I played one of Fagin's gang of street urchins in a community theater production of *Oliver!* Stole the show, too, when I burst into tears on opening night."

"Oh, no!"

"Not a very auspicious beginning." Jeff grimaced. "Fortunately I've learned to restrict my dramatic moments to those in the script. I've been onstage pretty consistently since then, always acting in one play or another.

"But now that I'm with the Limelight, I feel I've finally come home. It's a fantastic group. All the people are—well, aren't we in luck. You're about to find out for yourself."

He gestured toward the front door of the restaurant. Miranda turned and saw that a group of four had just come in, talking loudly and laughing as if they were the best of friends.

"Over here!" Jeff called, standing up.

"Jeffrey! What a lovely surprise!" A woman in her late forties or fifties, flamboyantly dressed in purples and blues, pranced toward them. "And who, may I ask, is this lovely creature?"

"Hopefully, a new member of the Limelight, Camille."

"Really? How wonderful. Barbara? Ted? Evan? Come over and meet David's latest victim."

"It's not definite yet," Miranda was quick to explain.

But as the four actors pulled up another table, meanwhile welcoming her and exclaiming over how pleased they were to meet her, she found herself wishing more than ever that Jeff's prediction would turn out to be true. By the time the meal was over, she felt so much a part of the troupe she could scarcely imagine her dream not coming true.

"That was fun," she said as Jeff walked her out of the restaurant, the two of them lagging behind the others. "I really enjoyed getting to know everybody."

"I hope you felt at ease. It's always hard, being the new kid on the block."

"I felt very comfortable. And I liked everybody."

"They're great, aren't they?" Jeff laughed. "A bunch of characters. But don't let them fool you. They're all terrific actors, every last one. You should have seen Camille's performance in *A Streetcar Named Desire*. She was the best Blanche Dubois you've ever seen."

They'd reached the corner then. Glancing at

her watch, Miranda saw she had only a few more minutes before she was due to meet Elinor.

"Thank you for lunch, Jeff," she said sincerely, turning to face him.

"No, Miranda. Thank *you*." His handsome features relaxed into a smile. "I'm glad I had this chance to get to know you a little." Jeff's green eyes were fixed on her intently. "I hope, in the future, I'll get to know you even better."

CHAPTER
17

Winter had come.

Darkness fell early, banishing the pale sun, draping thick folds of black over the washed-out gray. The only sign of life was the cedars, standing tall and proud even in the harshest winds, the dark green needles of the evergreens the only color in a collage of grays, blacks, and icy shades of white.

Tonight the full moon rose early, casting its light upon the desolate ground.

He lay on the cold stone floor in the basement of Cedar Crest, waiting. Knowing the change would soon come upon him. Hoping that, this time, he could triumph over the evil power.

Even before the night had fallen, he had descended into the depths of Cedar Crest. The cellar was uninviting, with its uneven floors and damp walls. Meandering hallways stretched out in all directions like an endless maze.

Still, this place alone offered sanctuary. A small room was tucked away down here. With its heavy wooden door that locked from the outside and only one small window covered with a metal grating, it resembled a cell.

He had locked himself in once before in his desire to control the beast's destructive urges. That other time, his attempts at containing the beast had failed. Someone had come from the outside. The girl, Corinne. She had opened the door, releasing him . . . and paying dearly.

This time, no one was likely to come.

In the center of the tiny room was the wolfsbane, a small clump of herbs tied together with string, the bright yellow flowers an odd contrast to the dreary room.

He lay next to it, hoping, listening to the library clerk's words echoing through his head.

The Native Americans believed wolfsbane warded off evil.

If only the legend were true. If only this really were the antidote.

If only this peculiar herb, with its strange, cheerful flowers, could keep him from shapeshifting.

"Please, *please*," he whispered, closing his eyes tight.

He opened them almost immediately. The full moon had moved across the sky so that it was shining through the window. Suddenly it cast its light onto his face.

And then he felt the tingling.

"No!" he cried aloud.

He reached for the wolfsbane, grabbing it in his fist and hurling it against the wall. The small cluster fell apart, nothing more than dried, useless weeds strewn across the stone floor, the bright blossoms suddenly seeming to mock him.

He shut his eyes again, not wanting to witness the change he so dreaded. Yet nothing could prevent him from feeling all the familiar sensations. The stretching of his limbs. The reshaping of his face.

The loosening of his grasp on the here and now.

Still, something was different this time. The change came upon his body just as it always had. But part of his mind remained as it always was.

This time the line between man and beast was thinly drawn.

And so the mighty animal was troubled as it paced about the basement room, its ears pricked, its nose picking up the subtlest of scents.

Tonight the urge to kill was strong.

The beast knew it would seek human prey.

The man resisted. Desperately it warned against killing a human being. Earnestly it fought the craving to hunt.

Yet the beast's urges were strong. It reared

up on its hind legs, pressing its sharp nose against the window. It could see the bars, thin strips of metal crisscrossed to form a grating, on the other side of the glass.

Suddenly it seemed a small obstacle to freedom.

Without hesitation the wolf struck the glass with its massive head. The window shattered into a hundred pieces, the jagged shards flying in all directions.

One small piece became lodged in the ruff of its neck. The beast shook it off distractedly. It had already turned its attention to the grating. In places, the iron was so rusted it had become dislodged from the window's edge. Removing it would be little challenge.

And so it hurled its head against the grating. It let out a yelp of pain, but paused for only a moment before trying again. After a few tries the corroded metal fell away, leaving a gaping hole. A hole that meant the beast's release. It sprang through the window, its sleek trunk just fitting through the small opening. It hesitated only a moment, getting its bearings before racing toward the forest.

At first it luxuriated in its freedom. It loped through the woods, leaping effortlessly over rotting logs, tearing through piles of wet leaves, careening around the maze of towering trees. But after only a short time, the battle raged once again.

Now that it was out in the wilds, instinct wrestled with what remained of the intellect. What the animal yearned for most, the man insisted was wrong.

To kill. To kill a human . . .

And then, suddenly, the wolf stopped. It stood frozen near a clump of marionberry bushes, sniffing curiously, one paw held in midair. It was picking up the scent of an animal—one it did not readily recognize.

Not a squirrel or a beaver. Neither moose nor elk nor deer.

Not a human.

And then it knew. Moving swiftly and silently through the forest, crossing the hostile terrain with grace and ease, it followed the scent. Its heartbeat quickened with anticipation.

The beast stopped when it came to the edge of a clearing. Through the middle bubbled a small stream, its water clear and fresh.

Crouching down behind a large bush, the werewolf lay in wait, watching as a large clumsy animal lumbered over to the edge of the stream. It reached a massive paw over the bank, craftily catching a fish. It devoured it in one quick swallow.

A bear. A grizzly, its fur thick and brown, its proportions monstrous, leisurely feeding on fish from the stream.

The werewolf watched in awe. Never before had it come across such a huge animal. The bear was easily one and a half times its own size, probably weighing three or four times what the wolf weighed.

Still, the werewolf sensed the bear would be no match for its strength.

Slowly it began inching toward its prey. When the time was right, it broke into a run.

The bear was caught by surprise. It turned at the sound of the approaching wolf, dropping the fish hanging from its mouth. Immediately it rose up on its hind legs. It towered above the wolf. As its enemy approached, with one giant paw it struck out.

The giant grizzly was quick and strong, the force of its blow enough to kill a man. But it did nothing to deter its foe.

The wolf paused only momentarily, wincing in pain from the scratches made by the bear's sharp claws. Angrily it went for the bear's side, clamping its jaws into its flesh. The bear let out a bellow that resounded through the forest like thunder.

The werewolf recoiled, then attacked once again. The bear let out another loud cry. Then it fell to the ground, its body hitting the forest floor with a thud.

The werewolf held back for a moment, not moving a muscle, barely breathing. And then it pounced one more time, this time going for the animal's throat.

CHAPTER 18

"Thanks again for coming," Miranda called, waving to Elinor through the open car window.

"Are you kidding? It was great. Thanks for inviting me! And if you talk to David Singer, thank him again for recommending that charming bed and breakfast." Elinor was walking toward the front door of her house, her overnight bag in her hand. "Bye, Miranda. I'll call you!"

As she backed out of the Clays' driveway, Miranda was exhausted from the long drive back. Her muscles ached and her eyes were so bleary she could barely focus.

But she was also exhilarated. Her day in Portland had convinced her that she belonged in the Limelight Theater Company. She wanted to be part of it so badly she wondered how she'd ever manage to wait to hear the results of her audition.

She was excited not only over the prospect of being onstage with such an excellent acting troupe, but also about being part of the corps of actors she'd met. She'd never met people like Jeff and the others. They were so self-confident. So motivated. So determined to experience life in the same way she longed to, by being in the center of things rather than simply sitting on the sidelines, watching.

As she wound around the curving streets of Overlook toward her house, she was already planning all the things she'd tell her mother about her stay in Portland. The audition, the people she'd met, the excitement of being in a city rather than her sleepy little hometown . . .

She turned one last corner onto her street. Instantly she stepped on the brake. Miranda's stomach tightened into a knot as the car lurched to a halt.

Parked in front of her house was a police car.

Miranda sat on the living-room couch, her legs drawn closely against her chest, her arms wrapped tightly around her knees. She kept her eyes fixed on the corner of the coffee table.

"Ordinarily, discovering a bear that had been mauled to death wouldn't have been a matter for the police," Officer Vale was saying. "It's just that it's such a bizarre coincidence, the way its wounds so closely match both those found on

Andy Swensen's body and those Corinne Davis suffered. It makes all three incidents that much more difficult to explain."

The police officer sounded very distant. Yet she was sitting in the chair opposite Miranda, only a few feet away. She was holding a pad of paper, opened to a blank page, a pen poised in the air.

"Elinor Clay filed a report not long ago," Officer Vale went on, her voice gentle. "She claimed that you and she encountered a wolf late one night, an animal that appeared to be vicious and out of control."

Miranda nodded. "A wolf," she said simply. "An ordinary wolf."

She knew Officer Vale would never accept the fact that a werewolf was responsible for the three gruesome attacks that had struck this small Oregon coastal town in less than two months' time, a town that had long ago forgotten the fears of the past, the danger. It was unimaginable. Yet despite her father's testimony that the attacker was probably an animal, Miranda was equally convinced the police officer would be able to believe that a secretive young man who'd recently come to Overlook, a loner with only a long-ago family connection to the town, with no friends except for Miranda, could well have been involved.

The last thing Miranda wanted to do was

raise her suspicions. So she was particularly on guard when the police officer sat down next to her and rested a friendly hand lightly on her shoulder.

"Miranda," she said in a kind voice, "I've been asking a lot of questions the last few weeks. And more than once, Garth Gautier's name has come up."

"A lot of people in this town don't like Garth." Despite her efforts not to, she knew she sounded angry.

"Why is that?" asked Officer Vale. "He's always seemed nice enough to me. That was my first impression when I met him that terrible night you two discovered Andy Swensen's body in the woods, and nothing that's happened since has changed my mind."

Miranda measured her words carefully. "Maybe it's because they don't know him. Because he's an outsider."

"Was he with you in Portland last night?"

The police officer asked the question so casually that it took Miranda a few seconds to realize its implications.

"Did Garth tell you he was?"

"I'm asking you."

Miranda was silent for a long time, her thoughts racing. Knowing what she knew had already forced her to make so many changes in her life. Altering her relationship with Elinor, throwing up barriers where before there were none. Forcing her to make a choice between pursuing her love of the theater and being there for Garth at a moment she knew he'd need her.

And now the police were involved. Did he expect her to lie? Had he given her as an alibi, saying he'd been out of town with Miranda the night of the third killing?

Miranda drew in her breath sharply. She didn't know how much he was implicated in this . . . if at all. But she did know how serious it was to lie to the police.

"No," she said, her voice so soft it was barely audible. "I went to Portland with Elinor Clay."

Officer Vale nodded. "That's what Garth told us."

A rush of air passed through Miranda's lips as the police officer stood up, flipping over the cover of her pad.

"There's just one more thing," she said. "I understand a classmate of yours, Mark O'Neill, got hurt playing with fire last Thursday."

"The whole school's been talking about it. He's in the hospital with second-degree burns."

"That's right. I spoke to him a few days ago. He claims the whole thing was just a stupid accident. He says he was showing off in front of his friend Dave Falco and things got out of hand."

"That's what I'd heard, too."

"Dave Falco's story is the same." Officer Vale

frowned. "The only thing that doesn't add up is the location of the accident. Both Mark and Dave claim they were up at Cedar Crest, but Garth claims he doesn't know anything about it."

Miranda started. "You spoke to Garth?"

"Yes. There are signs of a fire up there—the entire carriage house is half burned to the ground. Garth said it was caused by stored chemicals igniting suddenly."

Officer Vale shook her head slowly. "The truth is, we don't have anything to tie Garth to anything that's gone on around here recently. As a matter of fact, we're still at square one, trying to make some sense out of all this. As for your father's claim that an oversize wolf is probably responsible for the two attacks in the woods . . . well, that just adds even more confusion."

She started moving toward the door. "I'll be going now. Thank you for your time, Miranda. We'll be in touch if anything else comes up."

It was over. Miranda had passed this round, gotten through it without giving anything away.

She wanted to feel relieved. Yet as she watched the police officer pull on her coat, she knew she had no right to feel anything even close to relief.

It wasn't really over at all.

Miranda came straight home after school and lay stretched across her bed, her face buried in the crook of her arm. Remembering the events of the morning, she kept waiting to cry, but there were no tears.

There was only a dull ache at the bottom of her heart.

He had struck again.

If only you'd been here, a voice scolded. *If only you'd stayed in Overlook . . .*

Then what? What if you had been here? another voice countered.

That second voice knew there was nothing she could do. She was powerless against the force that drove Garth, making him attack . . . making him kill.

What was even more horrifying was the way she was drawn to it. Even as she was repelled by what he had done, a small part of her envied his freedom. She yearned for the exhilaration she now knew accompanied shapeshifting. Racing beneath the full moon. Reveling in the strength of her muscles, the power of her senses, the agility of her limbs.

Experiencing the glory of the hunt.

Miranda closed her eyes and lay back on the bed. In her mind she replayed the sensations she herself had experienced only a few days earlier. She inhaled the acrid odor of the decaying bark of a fallen log. Her ears reverberated with the sound of the wind whistling through the spiny needles of the towering cedars. The nerves in her arms and legs twitched as she remembered sailing over a pile of craggy rocks. . . .

"Miranda!" Her mother's voice put an abrupt end to her reverie. "Come downstairs. There's someone here to see you."

Miranda was surprised to find Selina at the bottom of the stairs. She was standing awkwardly in the front hall, her coat still on.

"Hi, Miranda," she said shyly, meeting her gaze for only a moment before lowering her eyes to the floor.

"Hello." Miranda hesitated. Her tone was guarded as she added, "Why don't you take off your coat and come in?"

As Miranda came down the stairs, Selina glanced up at her, her large green eyes soulful. "I wasn't sure if you'd want to see me."

"Selina, I . . ." Miranda let her voice trail off. "Let's go into the living room and sit down. Would you like something to drink?"

"No, thanks. I'm not going to stay long." She perched on the edge of a chair, keeping her coat on. "I came over because I heard about what happened. The way the police came to your house and all. . . . Oh, Miranda, I'm so sorry they've involved you in this!"

"Thank you, Selina. It has nothing to do with you."

"Doesn't it?" She bit her lip. "I can't help thinking that maybe some of the things I've said in the past got back to the police. You know, about Garth being an outsider, somebody nobody around here knows very much about. . . ."

"It's all right, Selina." Miranda was sincere. "I never blamed you for a moment."

"Thanks, Miranda." She took a deep breath. "Listen, there's something I've been wanting to say to you. I'm kind of nervous, so let me just get it out, okay?"

Miranda nodded.

"I know I've been really awful these last few weeks. Siding with Corinne when both of you went after the same part in the play, joining forces with Amy against you . . . I wasn't being fair to you, Miranda. I was letting other people tell me what to do, even though I never felt quite right about it.

"And, well, I want to apologize. And I want you to know that your friendship is still important to me."

"What about your friendship with Amy?" The words popped out before Miranda had a chance to think about them.

"Amy hasn't turned out to be much of a friend. I don't like the way she pits people against each other. And I certainly don't like the way she's been acting toward you. It took me a while to understand what she was doing . . . but I understand it now.

"Oh, Miranda, can you ever forgive me for

the way I've acted? Do you think we could go back to being friends—real friends?"

"Of course I forgive you. And I want us to be friends, too." Smiling, Miranda leaned over and gave her a big hug. "Oh, Selina, you don't know how glad I am that you're back!"

As soon as Selina left, Miranda climbed onto her bicycle. She felt as if a weight had been lifted from her heart. She was so pleased that Selina had come over . . . and that she had trusted her enough to share her true feelings about what had gone on between them over the past weeks.

Despite her optimism over the future of their friendship, a dark cloud hovered overhead. She was troubled by the visit from the police—and their report of another attack on the outskirts of Overlook. She wanted to see Garth, her desire to see him so strong it was almost a craving. She knew he was involved, and she wanted to help.

The ride out to Cedar Crest seemed endless. The wind whipped through her hair, blowing dark wavy strands into her eyes. Impatiently she pushed them away, wanting to concentrate on scaling the steep hills that separated her from him.

He was waiting for her. The front door was open, inviting in the chill winds of the bleak November day. He stood inside, his broad shoulders slumped, his tousled blond head bent forward in defeat.

"Garth." She went over to him and encircled his waist with her arms, drawing him close. For a long time she stood leaning her head against his shoulder. When she finally pulled away, she planted one light kiss on his lips, then another.

"You heard." His voice was flat.

Nodding, Miranda said, "The police were waiting for me when I got back from Portland."

"The police came to you, too? Oh, Miranda. I never wanted any of this to—"

"Sh-h-h. None of that matters." Gently she placed a silencing finger against his lips. "What about you, Garth? Are you all right?"

He hesitated before slowly pulling up his shirt. Huge welts marred the smooth skin covering his ribs, five bright bands of red.

Miranda gasped. "What happened?"

"The bear." He grimaced.

"Oh, my." She reached out, tentatively running her fingertips along the gashes. Garth winced.

"I want to make it better for you." She spoke in a hoarse whisper, her eyes filling with tears. "If only there were some way—"

She looked him squarely in the face, then wiped her tears with her fingertips. Still gazing up at him, she knelt down. She raised the fabric of his shirt, then brought the tips of her fingers gently down on the gashes, touching them ever so softly.

"Miranda." Finally he reached for her, placing his hands on her shoulders and pulling her upward. "My love."

As she rose, she caught a glimpse of the taut skin of his muscular torso.

The wounds had vanished.

"Garth, look!"

He glanced down, his face lighting up with amazement.

"You're magic," he said reverently.

"*We're* magic." She cradled his face in her hands. "It's strong, Garth. Strong enough for us to fight this. And I know what we must do next. There is someone who can help us—someone wise. But first, there's something I have to show you. Will you come? Will you let me lead the way?"

He placed the palm of his hand lightly against her cheek. "You are my strength, Miranda. You are my soul."

Miranda's mother was out, she discovered as she let herself into the house. The silent rooms seemed eerie, her voice echoing through them as she called hello.

"It's upstairs," she told Garth, taking him by the hand. "I was saving it, thinking I might give it to you as a present."

"What is it, Miranda?"

"A knife." She took a deep breath. "I found it

at a peculiar little shop in Norton, a store I'd never noticed before. It's special, Garth. There are two wolves carved into the wooden handle. One of them looks vicious, the other is simply staring—"

"Two wolves?" Garth, only halfway up the stairs, stopped in his tracks.

"Yes. Why, Garth? What does it mean?"

"The vision. The one I had the night of the play."

Understanding washed over Miranda. "Of course! The two werewolves! Oh, Garth, do you think the picture carved into the handle of the knife has something to do with what you saw?"

He frowned. "I'll know when I see it. The image from that night is etched into my brain so strongly I don't think I could ever forget it."

"Featherwoman was convinced the knife was important. I have no idea how she knew I had it, but she was outside the shop right after I bought it."

"What did she say, Miranda? It's important that you remember."

"She said I'd taken an important step. That this was the way it must be." She took a deep breath. "She said it was my destiny, that what had been set in motion couldn't be stopped."

Garth's lips were drawn into a straight line. "She knows."

Miranda nodded. "Yes. She has known all

along, ever since the beginning. I see that now. And that's why we must go talk to her."

They hurried up the stairs. Miranda went straight to the bottom of the closet, where she'd stashed the knife the evening of Bobby's party.

"I hid it in here," she told him as she rummaged around. "I didn't want my mother to see it. I wanted to protect her. . . ."

"Yes." Garth reached over and placed his hand on her shoulder. "I know how you must feel."

She didn't respond. She was too busy moving things around at the bottom of her closet. Panic was rising up inside her.

"I'm certain I put it in here—"

"Maybe I can help."

Miranda shook her head. "It was in a box. A big cardboard box filled with old things I hardly use anymore. Old clothes, mostly."

Garth knelt down beside her. "Here. Let me have a look."

"It's no use," she said, glancing up at him from where she was crouching. Her voice was edged with hysteria. "Garth, the box is gone!"

CHAPTER
19

The pale yellow sun was low in the sky as Miranda led Garth through the woods, toward a clearing. There Featherwoman's cottage was nestled. A blustery wind had risen up from the sea, turning the air bitterly cold, whipping around the stark, black branches of the trees.

Taking care not to stumble as she made her way through the most untamed sections of the forest, she thought back to the first time she'd come in search of Featherwoman. Miranda had been only ten years old then, a fifth-grader determined to do well on her first research paper. The topic she'd chosen was Overlook's most distinctive landmark, the totem pole in the center of town. And she'd sought out the one person she was convinced would know the most about the area's Native American history.

She remembered how nervous she'd been.

And the newness of the task she was undertaking was only part of it. Featherwoman's peculiar abode had long been the subject of rumor and speculation, especially among the impressionable young students at the elementary school. Some of them believed it was a magical place. They spoke about it in whispers, claiming the house stood on animal legs instead of a foundation of brick or concrete. That it vanished at nightfall, leaving nothing behind but a thin trail of smoke. That anyone who dared venture near it would fall under a curse, immediately being turned into a stubby bush like those that surrounded it.

Miranda hadn't believed any of it. But even she, the bravest of the fifth-graders, had been taken aback the first time she laid eyes on the house. It had struck her as strange . . . almost frightening.

Now she was going back. And she was bringing Garth with her. She wondered how he would react. As she stepped over a log, so decayed it was crumbling, she caught sight of the house through a clump of trees.

It was a small, squat, run-down structure, made of wood. What made it remarkable was the way in which it was painted. Native American designs in black and a dark shade of red stood out boldly against the nondescript brown background. There were some shapes that were clearly animals, fish and otters and eagles. Others looked like human faces.

She heard Garth draw in his breath sharply as he saw it for the very first time. Miranda reached over and took his hand before leading the way to the front door.

There was no need to knock. Featherwoman opened the door as they drew near. Her face registered no surprise. Instead, she moved out of the way, beckoning for them to come in.

"Come in, my children," she said. "I've already put the kettle on for tea."

Miranda rubbed her hands together as she stepped through the doorway. It was warm inside, thanks to a fire burning in the fireplace. It provided the only light in the room, casting stark, angular shadows everywhere. She blinked a few times to adjust to the dimness. Then her eyes darted around in an effort to take in her surroundings.

The inside of the house was as unusual as the outside. It consisted of one main room, bare of carpeting or paint or other such niceties. The walls, floors, and ceiling were natural wood. There were few pieces of furniture: a rough-hewn table, some simply crafted benches, three or four chairs gathered around the fireplace.

Everywhere there were Native American artifacts. Miranda remembered them from the last time she'd been here. What she'd forgotten was how wonderful they were, unlike anything else she'd ever seen. Huge tribal masks, grotesque exaggerations of human faces painted with bold strokes and trimmed with feathers or bits of fur. Great animal skins, treated in such a way that they had a texture similar to an artist's canvas and painted with symbols, the effect puzzling yet eerily beautiful. Wood carvings, mostly in the shapes of animals, ranging from crude to almost lifelike.

Part of her was unsettled by the presence of so many human and animal forms, all of them distortions of reality. But even more, Miranda was fascinated. The room seemed alive, not only with the present but also with the past. And not only was the human experience represented here; that of the animals, and all of nature, was as well. And there was one more dimension: here in Featherwoman's abode, the natural co-existed comfortably with the supernatural.

"You may look around," said Featherwoman. She was at one end of the large room, standing very still, watching. "Ask any questions you please."

Miranda, suddenly self-conscious, perched on the edge of a chair. She didn't feel comfortable poking around someone else's house. Of course she had questions. Many of them. Questions were what had brought her here today. But she was willing to be patient.

Garth joined her, pulling his chair up even

closer to the fireplace. He cast her a look that reflected what she was feeling: intense curiosity about everything that was around them both, combined with a strong hopefulness that somewhere amidst all these mystifying artifacts, and the legends that went with them, there might be something—anything—that would be of use to them.

Featherwoman disappeared behind a curtain for a few minutes, returning with a tray. On it were three cups of steaming tea. She came toward her guests silently, padding across the wood floor on feet enveloped by soft, beaded moccasins. The fire gave her brown leathery skin an orange tinge. Her jet-black eyes were fixed upon Miranda as she sat before her and Garth, cross-legged on the floor.

"You have come on a quest." It was a statement, not a question, spoken in a flat voice as she handed them their cups of hot tea. "There is something you need to know."

Garth nodded. "Please, Featherwoman. If you'll let us tell you what's been going on—"

"I think Featherwoman already knows." Miranda spoke softly. "You do know, don't you?"

The old woman gave a nod of her head. She paused to take a sip of tea. Then, after setting the cup on the floor, she folded her hands in her lap. She began to speak, her voice barely audible, her words deliberate.

"There is much I have to tell you. There is much you need to know. I will go back to the beginning, to the point at which it all began.

"Since the dawn of time, since the earliest records carved into the rocky walls of caves, the members of my tribe were known as great hunters. We lived mainly off the sea, killing whales and sea otters and fish. We made canoes from the tall cedars that grew so abundantly. We carved them with care, then painted them elaborately, using designs from nature and images from what you would consider the supernatural.

"My people lived very closely with nature. We were at one with the forests. With the seasons. And especially with the animals. There are many legends based on the animals of this region: the otter, the beaver, the eagle . . . and most of all the wolf. The wolf has always been believed to possess the greatest power, the strongest ties to the supernatural world.

"You see, my people also believed very strongly in the existence of beings from another world. That they coexist with us, playing a large part in our everyday lives."

Featherwoman was speaking more quickly, her voice growing more animated as she continued. "Like the people of many of the other tribes of the Pacific Northwest, mine believed we were descended from a child found drifting on a bed of kelp. This child was special. He was born of a supernatural being, then sent to us to be reared by our chief as his own son.

"My people knew this legend well. We recorded it in our paintings and in our carvings." Featherwoman stood up then, going over to the mantelpiece above the fireplace. Taking down a crudely made wood carving, she studied it in the flickering light of the flames. She was silent for a long time.

Miranda went to her and peered over her shoulder. At first glance, she saw only a piece of cedar that had been fashioned into a peculiar shape. Then, slowly, she was able to make out a human form. It was a baby, lying on a mound of seaweed.

When Featherwoman began speaking again, her voice was low. To Miranda, she seemed to be in a trance. Yet it was clear she knew exactly what she was saying, her words clear and carefully measured.

"And then, back during the time the Frenchmen first arrived, nearly two hundred years ago, the legend came true for the second time. A baby arrived. He was only a few days old when he drifted in on a bed of kelp. It was early in the morning. The hunters were getting into their canoes, readying themselves for a day at sea, when one of them spotted him.

"The tribe knew right away this was a supernatural being. That he had been sent to us from another world. Even the *tekijek*, the water monsters, the huge squids and the sharks and the devilfish with their otherworldly powers, had known to leave him alone. This, we knew, was the second coming of our ancestor. He was clearly meant to be adopted by the chief and raised as his own son. And that is what happened. The chief was a kind man, a good and fair ruler of the tribe. He called the boy Second One."

"The tribe must have worshipped him," Garth observed. "Believing that baby was a sort of god, that he had been sent to them—"

"Ah." There was a terrible sadness in Featherwoman's voice. She went over to one corner of the room. Propped up there was a rolled-up piece of parchment, tied with a bit of leather. After sitting down in the same place, she opened it, laying out what looked like a large animal skin on the floor in front of her. Painted on it in red were horrifying images: a snarling wolf, shown again and again, each time attacking a different creature. In most of the pictures, the animal's prey was human.

Miranda shivered. The look on the wolf's face was the same one she'd seen on the animal carving on the totem pole: a cruel grimace, its teeth bared and its eyes glowing menacingly.

"From the time he was a little boy, Second One was arrogant and evil. At first it was believed he was simply spoiled. It was true that the chief lavished all manner of special favors and gifts upon the boy. All the members of the tribe saw it, and so no one was surprised that the boy put himself above everyone else.

"But when he turned fifteen, something else happened."

Miranda felt Garth stiffen.

"At that age, it became clear that Second One's supernatural powers included the ability to change into a wolf."

"Werewolf." Garth said the word under his breath, so softly it came out like a sigh.

"We had always believed we had been born of the wolf. We called ourselves the Wolf Clan. And so we were not surprised when Second One proved able to shift from man into wolf. It was part of the narnauks' power, part of being so closely intertwined with nature.

"But Second One used his powers in evil ways. The change came only when the moon was full. Dark-haired from birth, he turned into a huge black wolf, so large and so powerful that no other living being could stand in his way."

Featherwoman pointed to the drawing of the dark wolf, its eyes a fiery gold that, even in the crudely made painting, glinted in a terrifying way.

"Second One ruled the Wolf Clan with an iron fist. He insisted that the terrifying image of a wolf—his own image—be put on every canoe, on every totem pole. He ignored the tribe's family traditions, taking many wives and fathering many children. He paid no heed to the laws by which we had lived. Instead, he created his own, harsh and merciless.

"All that was while he was in the form of a man. Whenever he was in the form of the wolf, he would seek out anyone who had dared to defy him. He would get his revenge. He killed many, many times."

Featherwoman closed her eyes. "And then, on the night of the first full moon after he'd turned eighteen, Second One killed the chief, the well-loved man who had acted as a father to him."

When she opened her eyes again, they were clouded. She shook her head slowly. "It was a dark time. There was so much suffering. So much killing. The evil narnauks had found in Second One an earthly being to carry out their most nightmarish deeds. The tribe had come to understand he was the narnauks' agent, sent here to do their bidding."

"Wasn't there anyone who opposed him?" Miranda asked. "Anyone brave enough to stand up to him?"

Silently Featherwoman walked over to the table, picking up a wooden carving. This one was made of a bleached wood, so pale it was almost white. It was a wolf—a fine, dignified animal, standing proudly with its front foot raised. It was the right paw. On it was a bright slash of white paint.

"White Foot." As Featherwoman said the name, her tone was one of reverence. "The oldest son of Second One.

"White Foot was as good as Second One was evil. Like his father, he had the power to change into animal form. Also like his father, he was believed to be controlled by narnauks. But while Second One was an agent of the bad narnauks, White Foot was an agent of the *good* narnauks.

"The two were at odds from the time White Foot was a little boy. If the child's mother hadn't stolen away with him one night, sneaking into a canoe and going off to live with another tribe, Second One surely would have killed him.

"But the boy survived. He grew into a man. And when he was eighteen years old he came back."

Featherwoman shook her head slowly. "It was a terrifying night. The moon was full, and both father and son had changed into animal form. Two powerful wolves—one white and one black, one good and one evil—faced each other for the final challenge."

A shiver ran down Miranda's spine. The image from the knife was flashing before her so clearly it was almost as if she held the carved wooden handle in her hand.

And then she remembered the knife was gone. Lost to her . . . even though Featherwoman had told her that finding it, having it in her possession, was part of her destiny.

"Those who witnessed the fight said it was the most horrible thing they had ever seen," the old woman continued. "Each of the wolves was empowered by forces stronger than what we mortals could ever understand. And they each fought to kill. The savagery, the snarling, the blood . . . it was a fight to end all fights."

"Who was the victor?" Garth asked, his voice a hoarse whisper.

"Ah. There was no victor. The battle between the good one and the evil one went on until both wolves were nearly killed. White Foot finally fled, barely escaping with his life. Some say it was because he realized he could never triumph over such a powerful force. He moved on to another region, where he was made chief of a new tribe. It is said he continued to use his special animal powers in a good way, finding food for his tribe even during the coldest of winters, killing their most fearsome enemies."

"And Second One?" asked Miranda.

"No one knows. Some say he vanished that night, hiding out in the woods to wait for a time when once again he could prevail. Others say he changed into a supernatural being, an evil narnauk who still lives in the icy blasts of winter, the treacherous storms that turn the sea black."

Featherwoman shook her head slowly. "There is one thing that all the stories about him acknowledge, and that is that his presence has never gone away. You see, Second One has not actually died. It has always been believed that it was only a question of time before he once again attempted to rule. To find some other earthly being to carry out his evil deeds. To allow the terrible darkness to fall over this region once again. This has been his terrible legacy."

"And you believe that Garth . . ." Miranda's voice trailed off. It was too horrible to speak about.

Yet the old Native American woman nodded her head. "Yes," she said. "Like so many Gautiers before him, Garth has been chosen by Second One to perpetuate his nefarious spirit. When the moon is full, he lives."

Miranda cast Garth a sidelong glance. He sat without moving, his breaths coming quickly, his expression dark.

Featherwoman's eyes grew narrow. "But we must fight it. *You* must fight it." She reached over and lay a leathery hand on each of them. "Together you will find a way."

"I—I don't know where to begin," Miranda said, holding her hands out helplessly.

"There are three things required to fight the evil power. I know by this insignia."

Featherwoman pointed to three lines, drawn amidst markings that were indecipherable to Miranda.

"What are they?"

Featherwoman cast her a calm look. "You will know when the time is right."

Once again Miranda thought of the knife.

"But what if I'm not able? What if I'm not strong enough?"

"You are not alone, Miranda. You must never forget that."

"But who—?"

"The good narnauks," Featherwoman said. "They are on your side."

"Are you sure they can protect her?" asked Garth, his voice thick with concern. "Are they strong enough? Can you promise me she'll be safe?"

As he spoke, a wonderful sensation suddenly swept over Miranda. She could remember experiencing the presence of the good spirits. It was the time she'd encountered Featherwoman in the forest, the day she'd gotten back her Native American necklace. She'd felt powerful, fearless, capable of anything.

Yet there was still so much uncertainty. So much she didn't know . . .

She reached over and took hold of Garth's hand. The same questions he had asked troubled her, as well, even in the face of the good narnauks' power.

"But how do I know their goodness is strong enough? How will I ever know the things I need to know?"

Featherwoman held up a silencing hand. "I can say no more, my child. All I can do is warn you not to ask for explanations for the things that cannot be explained.

"Have faith, my child. You must believe. Accept the fact that you are part of a destiny greater than anything you are presently able to comprehend."

Miranda was silent as she and Garth left the clearing surrounding the Native American's cottage. Featherwoman's predictions continued to echo through her head. She felt as if she were starring in a drama that was being played out in a realm far beyond any she had ever known before.

"We need to talk," Garth said, the sound of his voice jolting her out of her ruminations. "When we get back to Cedar Crest—"

"Garth," she said, gently placing her hand on his arm, "I want to go home."

"All right. I'll come with you."

Miranda hesitated. She needed time to think. Time to absorb the tale Featherwoman had told. Most of all, time to gather up the strength she now sensed she would be needing.

"No," she said. "I need to be alone."

She glanced at him and saw that his expression of surprise quickly changed to one of understanding.

"Whatever you want, Miranda," he said simply. "Whatever you need."

It was late by the time they said good-bye, clinging to each other in a long embrace before parting. As Miranda headed toward her house, the dark blanket of night was being drawn across the sky—black, starless, forbidding. She contemplated taking the longer route back to her house, the one that took her through town. But she wanted to beat nightfall, and so she headed into the woods.

As she walked, Featherwoman's words continued to haunt her. Even more, she was overwhelmed by the mission she now knew lay before her. It was her destiny . . . a destiny that could not be denied.

Miranda was well acquainted with the sounds of the forest at dusk: the frantic scurrying of small animals seeking shelter for the night, the high-pitched whistling of the evening breezes, the shushing of the tall cedars as they swayed to and fro.

And so she froze when she heard a sound she immediately knew didn't belong. It was a footstep. A heavy thud, the tread of someone or something weighty. It was behind her, back behind a particularly dense clump of trees. And it was close.

Miranda whirled around. "Who's there?"

She was greeted only by silence. Silence broken by the shriek of the wind, growing stronger and stronger as it rose off the sea.

Her first thought was the horsemen. Yet she knew instinctively they were not near. Their arrival had been greeted by a monstrous roll of thunder, swelling up out of the earth, and a putrid smell that stung her nostrils.

She forced herself to go on. The shadows were getting darker, deeper, swallowing up the gnarled trees that surrounded her. Miranda walked more quickly, taking care not to stumble and fall.

The snapping of a branch, just a few feet behind, sent a rush of adrenaline through her body, as sudden as a jolt of electricity. Her senses were unnaturally acute, her temples pounding from the blood rushing through her veins.

She was tempted to break into a run, wondering how far she'd get. The terrain was uneven and covered with vines and jagged rocks. The light was fading quickly. Still, it might be the best means of getting away. . . .

"I know you."

The sound of a human voice, deep and gravelly, made her stop in her tracks. She turned, more curious than fearful. Standing there, a few feet behind her, was a man. His hair was long and wild, coarse strands of black streaked with white, the same colors as his bushy beard. His nose was crooked, like a beak, his skin dark and leathery. He was dressed in a heavy wool coat, and there was a red-and-black plaid hunting cap pulled down over his head.

"Who—who are you?" she demanded. Yet she knew. The man Garth had mentioned, the one who'd accosted him at the theater, the night he'd had the vision . . .

"I've been watching you."

The man drew nearer. Automatically Miranda backed away. She was terrified. A voice inside told her to run. Yet she remained frozen to the spot, the muscles in her legs refusing to listen to reason.

"You went to the old woman's house."

"Featherwoman." Miranda stared at him, wondering how he knew where she had gone . . . and why he cared.

"You want her help. You need something from her."

"No, I—"

He took another step toward her. His face was close to hers. She could feel his breath against her cheek.

"I can help. I know things, too. She ain't the only one—"

All of a sudden Miranda's body was under her command once again. Without even thinking about what she was doing, she took off. She ran blindly, desperately, knowing only that she had to get away.

As she fled, the image of the man's face was fixed in her brain. The sound of his voice, as well: rasping, low, threatening. The memory was so clear it seemed as if he were still standing before her.

And the words he had spoken. They echoed through her brain: "I can help. I know things, too."

The man filled her with terror. Yet through her fears, through her instinctive urge to flee what was so foreign, so frightening, came a realization: that this man could well be speaking the truth.

CHAPTER 20

It was comforting, emerging from the forest and into her own backyard. The lights shining inside her house were bright and friendly, a welcome change from the all-consuming darkness of the wintry night. Her agitation over her encounter with the strange man in the woods was already fading as she trudged up the back steps. She was home.

She found her mother in the kitchen. Mrs. Campbell was humming as she bustled about, preparing dinner. Enticing smells filled the room. A wooden cutting board was piled high with chopped vegetables, carrots and celery and onions.

"Hi, honey," her mother said, glancing over her shoulder. She didn't stop stirring the sauce on the stove. "Dinner will be ready in a half hour."

"What are you making?" She planted a kiss on her mother's cheek, meanwhile peering over her shoulder.

"Something new. I found it in a French cookbook I got out of the library. It's funny; after weeks of not wanting to be bothered with cooking, I'm suddenly finding it fun to experiment."

"I don't suppose this has anything to do with the way you and Daddy are spending so much time together lately, does it?"

Mrs. Campbell just smiled.

"Mom," Miranda said, suddenly thinking of the missing knife, but trying to sound casual, "Have you seen that box of old clothes I'd been keeping at the bottom of my closet?"

"I've been meaning to do a major cleaning for ages. Finally I had a burst of energy—"

"What did you do with it?"

Her mother looked up, clearly surprised by the intensity of her tone. "Honey, those clothes have been sitting around for months. Most of them didn't even fit you anymore—"

"Where's the box, Mom?"

"I took it to the thrift shop in Norton. Miranda, if there was something in there you still want, I'm sure you could go over to the store and buy it back. Or maybe if you explain to them—"

Without giving her mother a chance to finish her sentence, she headed toward the back door.

"Miranda, they're probably closed by now!"

her mother called after her. But Miranda paid her no heed.

Pushing hard against the pedals of her bicycle, Miranda did her best to quell her rising panic.

"Why wasn't I more careful?" she scolded herself, speaking out loud even though there was no one to hear except the wind.

Still, she was heartened by the possibility that maybe, just maybe, she might be able to get the knife back.

She made it to Norton in record time, then found the thrift shop without any trouble. It was on Moss Avenue, in the middle of the block. She didn't even bother to lock up her bike; she simply leaned it against the building and dashed inside.

There were only two or three customers in the small store, perusing the racks of used clothing or examining the shelves of toys and housewares.

Miranda barely gave them a glance. Instead she headed for the woman standing behind the counter, rearranging the earrings and bracelets on the tray of jewelry she'd taken out of the glass display counter.

"Excuse me," Miranda said breathlessly.

"I'm sorry, miss. We're about to close." The woman glanced toward the clock on the wall.

"Please, if you'll just give me a minute." She

took a few seconds to get her bearings. "My mother donated a carton of clothes the other day, and there was something at the bottom of the box that I need."

The woman frowned. "Oh, dear. We've had so many donations lately. . . . Here, I'll show you."

She stepped toward the back of the shop, gesturing for Miranda to follow. Behind a closed door was a room, bare of furniture except for the long narrow tables that lined the walls. They were piled high with an odd assortment of goods: clothes in a rainbow of colors, well-worn shoes, toasters and sleds and rubber boots. In one corner were cardboard boxes, stacked so high they threatened to topple over at any moment.

Miranda's heart sank.

"This is what's come in over just the past three days." The woman sounded apologetic. "You're welcome to look through it, if you'd like, although I really am about to lock up. . . ."

"Is this everything that's come in recently?" Miranda's voice betrayed her despair.

"Well, most of it."

Startled, Miranda glanced at her. "What do you mean?"

"As the boxes come in, a couple of volunteers sort through the donations. They weed out anything they don't think we'll be able to sell.

And if the cartons are torn or in bad shape, they toss them into the Dumpster out back."

The woman thought for a moment. "There are always a few things that get left behind in the truck. You know, the one that picks up donations at people's homes. You'd be surprised how many things fall out of the cartons. Or sometimes an entire box just collapses. . . ."

She cast Miranda a rueful look. "I'm sorry I can't be more helpful. It's just that we're constantly getting new things in. And because we're all volunteers, and most of us just work here a few hours at a time, there's a constant changeover of personnel."

Miranda had begun moving about the room, poking through the piles of clothing, peering into boxes. The glimmer of optimism she'd been feeling not long before was fading fast.

"Exactly what is it you're looking for?" the woman asked.

"A knife."

"If you wait a few days, you might be able to find it in our housewares section."

Miranda shook her head. "It's not that kind of knife."

She thought for a moment. Then, exasperated, she asked, "Do you think I could draw a sketch of it and you could leave it near the cash register? I'm even willing to offer a small reward. If one of your volunteers, or even one of your customers, were to come across it . . ."

"I think we could do that." As the woman made her way back to the counter, she turned back. "It's really important, isn't it?"

Miranda just nodded.

Miranda sat at her desk at school, her eyes traveling to the clock every two minutes. She wasn't at all able to focus on the lecture given by her history teacher. Since the night before, she'd been distracted. It began when she was riding home from Norton, defeated after the episode at the thrift shop.

All around her, she'd been surrounded by the night.

Suddenly she was struck by an overwhelming urge to be close to the wolfskin. To touch it, to feel its weight upon her shoulders . . . to experience the same exhilaration that she had known once before. She'd barely slept all night, still haunted by her all-encompassing desire.

Immediately after school, she headed straight for her bicycle, taking care to avoid Elinor and Selina and everyone else she knew. She tossed her schoolbooks into the wicker basket and climbed on, riding away at a frenzied pace. The lure of the wolfskin was becoming more and more irresistible. It was no longer a desire; it was a need.

She veered into the parking lot of the town

library, certain it must be back at the library by now. Garth had to have returned it. He'd been ambivalent about her shapeshifting from the very beginning; surely he'd have been anxious to get rid of it.

As she locked her bike outside the brick building, she was completely out of breath. Her chest was sore from the exertion of the ride, and beads of perspiration ran down her forehead. She didn't care. Nothing mattered except returning to the place in which the wolfskin was stored.

The town library was quiet. Two older men sat opposite each other in the periodicals section, one reading a magazine, the other that day's newspaper. Several people were standing among the stacks, studying the books lined up on the shelves. A few high school students sat at one table toward the back, working on a group project. Miranda, recognizing them, waved, then quickly moved toward Ms. Wallace.

The library clerk was talking on the telephone. Miranda tried to hide her impatience as she waited. By the time she got off the phone, one of the older men, the one who'd been reading the magazine, had come up to the counter.

"Yes?" Ms. Wallace looked at Miranda questioningly.

"I was wondering if I could go into the museum downstairs."

The clerk frowned. "That place is such a mess. You know we're packing up all the exhibits—"

"Excuse me," the man interrupted. "I wonder if you have any back issues of—"

"You'll have to wait your turn," Ms. Wallace told him firmly.

"I know you're closing up the museum," said Miranda. "But if I could just go down for a few minutes. Please . . ."

"All I need to know," the man interrupted once again, "is whether or not you have old issues of this magazine."

Ms. Wallace sighed. "They should be on the shelf, sir. Right underneath the display rack."

"I looked, but I didn't see them. If you wouldn't mind, I'd appreciate it if you'd take a look."

The clerk sighed. "If you'll just give me a minute, sir—"

"I have an idea." Miranda tried to keep the excitement out of her voice. "Why don't you give me the keys, and I'll just go down by myself? That way, you won't have to bother." Pointedly, she added, "I can see how busy you are."

Ms. Wallace cast the man an annoyed glance. Then she reached into her skirt pocket, coming up with a ring of keys. "Here. This key unlocks the door. Just don't touch anything!"

The corridor in the basement was shadowy,

illuminated only by the light from the stairway. After cautiously making her way to the end, Miranda fumbled with the lock for some time before she managed to get the door open. Her heart was pounding. The yearning to be near the wolfskin was so strong she was dizzy.

And then the door was open. She flicked the switch on the wall. Instantly the room was bathed in glaring fluorescent light. It took her eyes only a moment to adjust. Her glance darted about the room, seeking out the glass display case in which the wolfskin was stored.

It was empty.

"No!"

A terrible sob rose up from deep within Miranda's chest. Desperate, she fell to her knees, the palms of her hands flat against the smooth glass of the display case.

Coming out of the library, Miranda felt shaken and out of control.

What's happening to me? she wondered as she made her way home, making a point of staying on the winding back roads of Overlook, keeping as far away from the forest as she could.

She tried to convince herself her craving to be near the wolfskin was due simply to her desire to learn more about shapeshifting, that it was rooted in her determination to understand Garth and the terrible curse that plagued him.

Leaning her bicycle across the garage and crossing the backyard, she made a pact with herself to ignore the feelings of dread that continued to gnaw at her.

Miranda was about to head inside the house when something caught her eye. It was a piece of white paper, wedged in between the back door and its frame. Curious, she pulled it out.

The paper was smudged with dirt. The handwriting was almost childlike, the letters, scrawled in pencil, large and uneven. It was a short note, only six words. But their meaning struck Miranda with all the impact of a physical blow.

I know where the knife is.

She knew instinctively who had left this note. The man's face was etched clearly in her mind. The dark eyes, burning into her; the wild mane of hair and the shaggy beard; the deep voice, sending a chill through her as he called to her, his voice cutting through the silence as sharply as a razor.

The man from the forest.

I know things, too.

She'd been frightened by him, reacting viscerally to his looming presence. Yet there was still the chance he was telling the truth. That maybe, just maybe, he could provide some answers, fill in the gaps of the puzzle whose solution continued to elude her.

Now she knew he had been telling the truth.

Instinctively she knew where to find him. It was a terrifying place, one she'd dreaded ever since she was a little girl. Yet she had to venture there. She had to take a risk . . . to reach deep inside herself and somehow overcome her own fears.

Grasping the note tightly in her hand, she understood that she no longer had any choice.

CHAPTER
21

Miranda reached out and grabbed hold of the spindly branch of a tree just in time to keep from stumbling. The path she was following was steep and winding, snaking up the side of one of the highest mountains around Overlook. Her sneakers kept slipping against the muddy spots, still wet from the late autumn rains. Sharp rocks jutted out at odd angles, making it slow going.

She'd never been up Broken Branch Trail before, even though she'd heard about it since she was a little girl. The difficulty of climbing it was well known. From early on children were warned to keep away from it, their parents instilling fear in them about its steep inclines and sudden drops.

Yet the physical demands of traveling the rugged, uphill path was only part of it. Even more, the warnings were rooted in the legends that surrounded it. They replayed in Miranda's mind as she climbed late Friday afternoon. They suddenly sounded terrifyingly plausible. One was that the trail led clear up to the stars. Another was that those who'd dared to climb it had seen things they could never bring themselves to speak about. Still another said that anyone who followed the trail to its end would never be seen again.

Yet she'd known intuitively this was where the man who'd left her the note lived. He'd come down off the mountain, a place of isolation, a refuge for those who wouldn't—or couldn't—live among others. And it had to be the mountain upon which Broken Branch Trail twisted and turned.

Miranda was tired by the time she reached the trail's end. Climbing it had, indeed, been a challenge. But she'd been determined. Now, gazing out as she paused to catch her breath, she saw that there was more to this place than a treacherous climb and a handful of legends. The view was magnificent.

From where she stood, Miranda had a clear view of Devil's End. The ocean seemed roughest there, its waves colliding violently with the harsh, rocky precipices. She watched for a while, hypnotized by the rhythmic crashing. The angry motion of the water was unsettling, and when she finally managed to look away, it was a relief.

She turned, heading across the flat surface of this part of the mountain. Not far in the distance, a curl of black smoke drifted up lazily from behind the trees.

His house.

Miranda swallowed hard. Her heart was pounding as she set off in that direction. Carefully she made her way through the forest's dense growth. For the first time since she'd begun, she wondered if she were making a mistake. Coming up here like this, all alone. . . .

And then she found herself in a clearing. It was a small patch of land, dotted with ragged tree stumps. In its center was a crudely made cabin, fashioned from rough wooden planks. They'd been hammered together in a haphazard fashion; the angles were slightly off, the ends not quite squared. The roof was tar paper. One of the windows was broken, its jagged edges jutting out like teeth.

Miranda would have assumed this cabin was abandoned except for the black smoke drifting out of the chimney, its sooty color a complement to the clouds splashed across the gray wintry sky. A yellow dog, so thin its ribs were clearly visible, came out from around back, staying just long enough to give her a woeful stare and let out a halfhearted bark before slinking away.

She stood outside the door, listening. From within came no signs of life. There was only silence. She wondered if she should turn and flee. Yet she'd come this far. . . .

She held up a hand, preparing to knock on the wooden door.

"Y'came."

Miranda whirled around, her hand still clenched into a fist.

"I knew y'would."

Standing a few paces away was the man. He'd come out of the woods, she realized, carrying a rifle at his side. He'd been watching her. Maybe even waiting for her. Or perhaps it was simply a coincidence.

Instinctively Miranda stepped back. Yet she did not avert her eyes. Instead, she looked at him closely for the first time. Her original impression had been accurate: he was a large, burly man, heavyset and strong. His appearance was ragged: his well-worn clothes disheveled, his white-streaked dark hair wild and long, his black beard badly in need of a trim.

But while the other time she'd seen him she'd seen a crazed look in his eyes, this time she saw kindness.

Suddenly Miranda's fear slipped away. She took a step toward him, reaching out her hand.

"Who are you?" she asked in a gentle voice. "How do you know so much?"

He gazed at her for a long time before saying, "Come inside, Miranda. This day's too cold and damp for you to be standing outside."

As he pushed open the front door of his cabin, Miranda peered through. She knew she should be cautious. But what she saw inside immediately allayed any lingering fears.

The man's family was sitting before the fire. A plain-looking woman—his wife, Miranda supposed—was reading to three small children in a soft voice. Her face was glowing, although whether it was from the flame's bright color or the love she felt for her children, Miranda couldn't tell. The woman was pretty, her long hair pulled back into a braid that reached nearly to her waist. Soft tendrils fell about her face. She glanced up at Miranda with large dark eyes, her face quickly melting into a welcoming smile.

"Come in," she greeted her. "You must be the gal my husband told me about."

"I'm Miranda Campbell."

The woman nodded, then turned to her three children. "Lesson's over for now. Go outside to the stream and fetch some water. Go on, now. All of you."

Miranda watched as the three children, none of them older than six or seven, scurried away. Like their parents, they were dressed in threadbare clothes. Even so, their faces radiated a kind of joy.

"I'm called Dominique," said the woman.

Glancing at her husband, she added in a teasing tone, "Knowing Augustus, he probably forgot to tell you my name."

Relaxing a little, Miranda told her, "Up until now, I didn't know your husband's name, either."

She glanced around the cabin, already getting accustomed to this place that had only moments before felt so strange and so forbidding. The few rooms were airy and bright, the light from the fire augmenting the grayness of the day coming in through the many windows. The uneven wooden floors were covered with hooked rugs handmade in rich earth tones, deep brown and forest green and the golden hue of the sun's rays. All the furniture looked handmade, odd, creative pieces fashioned from the cedar trees that covered the mountain. The children's artwork was tacked up all around, bright finger paintings and collages made with a variety of textures and colors.

While the simple cabin emphasized that these people had very little, this was a warm and friendly home. Miranda reflected on how odd it was that not long before she'd actually been afraid of Augustus. Now she saw him as a caring man who'd chosen a modest life for himself, a kind man who'd surrounded himself with a loving family.

"I'll git you some apple cider," Dominique offered, rising from the wooden rocking chair in which she'd been sitting. Draped across the back was a handmade quilt. "You must be parched, after climbing up this mountain. It ain't easy, gittin' to our place."

"Y'know what the folks around these parts call this mountain?" Augustus asked. He lowered himself onto a wooden chair made from thick branches tied together with strips of leather.

Miranda shook her head.

With deliberate movements he reached into his jacket pocket and took out a pipe and a pouch of tobacco. "We call it Goater's Bluff."

"Were there goats living on this mountain once?"

"Nope." He'd begun the painstaking process of filling his pipe with cherry-scented tobacco. "Legend has it that the original name was Gautier's Bluff."

Miranda heart fluttered. "Gautier," she repeated in a hushed voice.

"That's right." There was an earnest look in his dark eyes as he added, "Had a feelin' you'd be interested."

"Tell me," Miranda said hoarsely. "Tell me everything you know."

Augustus lit his pipe, then took a long, slow puff. He nestled back more comfortably into his chair.

"The reason this mountain's called Goater's

Bluff, or Gautier's Bluff, is that 'bout two hundred years ago, a man who went by the name of Louis Gautier got himself quite a reputation around these parts."

"Who was this man?"

"A fur trapper. It was back in the late 1780's that the first French explorer came here to the Pacific Northwest. La Pérouse was his name. No doubt he'd heard tell of the European seafarer, Captain James Cook, who, a decade earlier, had started trading with the tribes around here, bringin' valuable furs back with him to England. Bear, fox, raccoon, wolf, and especially otter.

"Wasn't long before a whole passel of other Frenchmen came, wantin' to cash in on the fur trade. One of 'em, the story goes, was a loner named Louis Gautier."

"Garth's ancestor," Miranda breathed. "What do you mean when you say he was a loner?"

"That he was one of those types that kept to himself. Y'know, as if he was keepin' a secret or something. . . ." Augustus's dark eyes narrowed. "Or maybe that he was somebody who felt more comfortable around the animals in these parts than around other people."

A chill ran down Miranda's spine. "Go on."

"This Frenchman, Gautier, quickly gained a reputation for himself as the finest trapper of them all. His kill was greater than any other man's. 'Fore long, some of the others grew suspicious. They were jealous, and they wanted to know how Gautier managed to outdo all of 'em.

"The way the story goes is that three of 'em, three Frenchmen, banded together and followed him one night. Two of 'em went mad right after. Never spoke a word of sense again, not either of 'em. But one stayed right in his mind. He wrote down what happened in a journal he kept."

"What happened?" The feeling of dread that had crept over Miranda as she listened had already told her what Augustus was about to say.

"There was a full moon that night. All three men trailed him, keeping far enough away that Gautier wouldn't see 'em. The forest was bright, lit up by the moon. They watched as he went into a clearing, standin' there as if he was waitin' for something. And then . . ."

He paused, averting his eyes. "He shapeshifted." Augustus swallowed hard. "Louis Gautier changed into a werewolf.

"At least, that's what it says in the man's diary. Like I said, the other two never could say whether he was fibbin' or not. Their minds weren't good for much after what they seen that night, whatever the truth of it was. Anyway, the man claimed that when Gautier took the form of a wolf, he killed them small animals quick and easy, better than any human could ever hope.

"He ran through the woods, swift and silent. He piled up the bodies of his prey in one place, at the foot of the mountain. The next day, he was back in the form of a man. He brought them to the post and traded 'em in." He chuckled before adding, "Quite a story."

"Do you believe the man saw what he said he saw?"

Augustus peered at her over his pipe. "Do you?"

He didn't wait for her reply. "After word got out about Gautier, everybody pretty much left him alone. Nobody knew if the story was true, but nobody really wanted to find out. This mountain had been his main hunting ground, and the others left it to him. Nobody ever made nothing official, but the other trappers never dared trespass on his territory again. That was when this mountain started bein' called Gautier's Bluff.

"Gautier stayed a loner until he took a wife, a beautiful Indian woman who lived around these parts. It was a love match, they say. The two of 'em moved up north, far away from where the others had settled. Wasn't much time gone by before they had a child. A son.

"But it wasn't long before Gautier's world was shattered. His wife took sick right after the baby was born. Something wasn't right. When she died, some said the bad narnauks carried her off, angry that she'd fallen in love with a French-man, somebody not of her own kind. The man was heartbroken. They say losing her made him a little touched in the head. Maybe it was that, or maybe he figured he'd never be able to take care of his son. Whatever it was, one day when the baby was only a few weeks old, he placed him on a bed of kelp and set him off into the ocean.

"Gautier no doubt expected him to drown. But instead the baby drifted down the Oregon coast to a settlement of Native Americans. The ones who lived at the foot of Goater's Bluff, right above Devil's End."

Miranda nodded. "Featherwoman's tribe."

"That's right." Augustus took a slow puff on his pipe. "When I saw you and Garth Gautier goin' there, out to Featherwoman's place, I knew you were startin' to put the pieces to-gether."

He leaned forward, looking her in the eye. The light from the fire caused his dark eyes to glow. "He does it, doesn't he?" It was more a statement than a question. "He changes. He changes when the moon is full."

"I . . . He . . ."

He held up his hand. "You don't have to tell me. I already know. I seen it myself."

Miranda gasped. "You have?"

"Man like me, makes his livin' off the woods in these parts, spends a lot of time out in the forests. All the time. Daytime . . . and nighttime. I been out there when he changed, Miranda. I seen it for myself." He was nodding as he said, "That's how I know the story 'bout that fur trapper is true. It's the Gautier family legacy."

Suddenly panic rose up inside Miranda. "You're not going to tell—?"

Augustus looked at her earnestly. "When I was a boy, I chose a life for myself that was apart from the rest of the world. I live on my own, Miranda. I live off the earth, botherin' nobody, hopin' nobody bothers me. I answer to my wife and my young'uns, and that's all. They're all I need. I keep to myself, and I wouldn't want anything but the same for other people."

Shaking his head slowly, he said, "You got nothin' to worry 'bout. Your secret is safe with me."

Just then Dominique came back into the room. In her hand was an earthenware pitcher. Steam rose out of the top.

"Hot apple cider," she said, smiling. "We picked the apples this fall. Couldn't hardly be tastier."

Miranda accepted the mug Dominique offered. Augustus took some, too, and the three of them sat in silence for a long time, sipping the hot liquid.

Finally he spoke. "I hope this was helpful to you, Miranda."

"Slowly the pieces are beginning to fit together," she replied. "First Featherwoman's story, now yours . . . The tale behind the Gautier family's horrible legacy is finally coming into focus."

Setting her mug down on the floor beside her, she added, "But there is one more thing. I still don't know how the curse began. Even more important, I don't know how to banish it."

Beside her, Dominique said softly, "You want to help Garth."

Choking on her words, Miranda told her, "I want to save him."

It wasn't until then that she remembered Augustus's note. "The knife!" she gasped. "You said in your note you know where the knife is!"

"That's part of it, isn't it?" he said. "It's what you need to remove the curse."

Featherwoman's words echoed through her head. "There are three things required to fight the evil power. . . ."

Miranda had come to realize the knife was one of them.

"Yes," she told Augustus. "We need the knife. Please, tell me how I can get it back."

His expression darkened. "I know where it is . . . but you can not git it back so easily."

"Where is it?"

"There's a stream that runs down Goater's Bluff. It starts way up top, comin' all the way down the side of the mountain, meanderin' all over this way and that. More than a mile long, easy, I'd say."

"The knife is in the stream?"

"I saw it there. Floating in the roughest part, where the stream goes 'round a bend. Tried to grab it, but the water was movin' too fast."

"How will I ever get it back?" Miranda cried.

Dominique reached over and placed her hand on her arm. It was warm and soft, giving instant comfort.

Yet there was something else that quelled Miranda's rising panic. All of a sudden that same feeling of peace she'd experienced before rose up inside her. A sensation of serenity, of strength . . . of certainty that, in the end, everything would work out for the best.

The good narnauks. She was learning about their power. Their benevolence surged through her, lifting her away from her fears.

Another thing Featherwoman had said came to her: "You will know when the time is right."

The knife was near. It had not vanished. Somehow, perhaps through some power she would never understand, it had found its way into the stream that ran down Goater's Bluff.

She felt heartened. For the first time since her quest had begun, she found herself believing that it *was* simply a question of faith. That all the elements she needed really would come together.

At that moment, sitting in the refuge that was Augustus and Dominique's home, Miranda trusted that, when the time was right, she would find inside herself the strength she needed to carry out her mission.

CHAPTER
22

Miranda was basking in the glow of optimism as she headed toward home early Friday evening. As she crossed her backyard she was lost in thought, ruminating about what Augustus had told her.

At last she understood the ties between the Native American tribes from this area and the Gautier family. It had begun with the arrival of a baby on the bed of kelp . . . a baby who was the son of a fur trapper, a man capable of shape-shifting into a wolf whenever the moon was full. Slowly, the entire sequence of events was coming into focus.

If only I knew how it began, she thought. How Louis Gautier's ancestors first began to shapeshift . . .

She was pondering this point as she let herself into the house through the back door.

Suddenly she started, snapped back into the present by discovering her parents sitting opposite each other at the kitchen table.

"Dad!" she exclaimed. "Is—everything all right?"

"Everything is just fine." Dr. Campbell held up his mug. "Want some coffee?"

"No, thanks." Miranda cast her mother a questioning look. She found her answer in the way her eyes were glowing. "I'll have a piece of that cake, though."

Miranda sat down at the table between her mother and her father. The cake, freshly baked, was a chocolate layer cake—her father's favorite. She cut herself a piece, keeping it small because she had the distinct feeling she was interrupting something.

"How's business?" she asked her father conversationally.

"The usual. Helped one of Dave Hawkins's cows deliver a calf about an hour ago."

"Everything all right?"

Dr. Campbell grinned. "Mother and baby are doing just fine."

"Oh, I almost forgot." Mrs. Campbell set down her coffee cup. "Selina called."

"Selina? Really?"

"She was wondering if you wanted to go to the movies this weekend."

"Sounds like fun." Miranda was speaking

more to herself than to her parents. "Maybe I'll ask Elinor to join us."

"Good idea." Miranda's mother hesitated. "I've noticed you two haven't been seeing very much of each other lately. But this is just like old times."

Just like old times. Her mother's words haunted Miranda as she quickly finished up her cake, deposited the plate in the sink, and went upstairs to call Selina back.

It *was* just like old times. Her parents sitting together in the kitchen, talking calmly, sharing a pot of coffee. A telephone call from Selina, suggesting the two of them take in a movie together. At that moment, it felt as if everything were the same as it had been weeks earlier—before her parents' separation, before the play and the resulting tension between her and her two oldest friends . . . before Garth.

Yet something was different. Something felt wrong.

Whereas back then Miranda's life had felt comfortable, complete, now—somehow—something was missing.

It was that same intense yearning she'd felt before, right after she'd gone into Norton in search of the missing knife. It came upon her now, as she stood on the stairway, clutching the wooden banister with both hands. The longing to shapeshift, to experience the freedom of running through the wild . . .

"*No!*" she cried aloud.

She had to resist. Already she had succumbed once, giving in to the desire to feel the wolfskin, to replay the scene that had never left her mind, not since she'd raced wild and free beneath the light of the moon.

Miranda stood very still, holding on to the banister, acutely aware of the wood beneath her fingers: its smooth texture, its coolness, its origins in nature, something wondrous that she, too, was part of. . . .

She realized that all her senses were suddenly hypersensitive. She could pick up the most subtle of smells. A bar of scented soap upstairs next to the sink, the lemon oil her mother had used to polish the furniture days earlier, even the chocolate cake, all the way downstairs in the kitchen. And her hearing was uncannily clear. She could hear the water dripping in the leaky bathtub, the coffeepot sighing, her father's fingertips drumming on the kitchen table.

And the restlessness. A burst of adrenaline set her heart pounding. Her blood rushed, throbbing violently through her veins. Her muscles twitched. Her jaw ached. She yearned to push herself to the limit—

The shrill ringing of the telephone burst through her reverie.

"I'll get it," she called automatically. She

raced up the stairs to the phone in the second-floor hallway.

"Hello?" She was out of breath. Miranda expected it to be Selina, or perhaps Elinor. And so she was completely taken aback by the low male voice with the lilting intonation that came across the wire.

"That clear, resonant voice could belong only to Miranda Campbell," said the director of the Limelight Theater Company. "Hello, Ms. Campbell. This is David Singer."

"Mr. Singer!" Miranda took a moment to compose herself. "How are you?"

"Just fine. I wanted to tell you personally that the lead in *La Rose* is yours—if you want it."

"If I *want* it?" She gasped. Then, realizing how she probably sounded, she stopped herself, taking a few deep breaths. After all, she was no longer a mere high school student daydreaming about the big plans she had for herself. She had just been invited to become part of a professional acting troupe.

"Yes, I want the part," she said with as much dignity as she could muster.

"Good. One of the other actors in the troupe will call you with the rehearsal schedule as soon as it's set."

Miranda's first impulse was to run back downstairs to tell her parents the good news. But something held her back. Part of her wanted to be alone, to savor this good news all by herself before inviting the other people in her world to share it.

She went into her bedroom and lay down. With her eyes closed, she tried to imagine what it would be like, being onstage with the other members of the Limelight Theater Company. Performing in Portland. Staying up all night after the play's debut, waiting up with the other cast members until the morning papers came out with the reviews.

She tried imagining the sound of the audience's applause. As she did, she waited for a rush of excitement to wash over her. Instead, there was another feeling, one that stubbornly refused to be pushed aside to allow this newer, fresher one to surface.

It was the same pull she'd felt on the stairway a few minutes earlier.

With a jolt, Miranda realized that beside the lure of shapeshifting, even having her dream come true paled.

She was overcome with confusion. She had worked so hard to make this moment happen. She had fantasized about it. She had written about it in her diary, pouring out her fears that what she so yearned for would never come true. Yet now that it had become a reality, she was unable to appreciate it, to experience her triumph in the way she'd always assumed she would.

You should be happy, she scolded herself. You're getting what you always wanted. The play. Your parents. Selina. Everything is going back to the way it used to be.

And then, in a flash, she realized what the real problem was.

Yes, everything was going back to the same way it had been before. The difference was that *she* was no longer the same.

She wanted desperately to see Garth.

After quickly telling her parents the good news about the Limelight Theater Company, Miranda jumped onto her bicycle and headed for Cedar Crest.

Garth will understand, she thought as she bumped over the uneven surface of Winding Way, the tires of her bicycle sending pebbles and particles of dirt flying. He knows. He must have felt this yearning. This desire. This irresistible, unconquerable longing to run with the wolves.

It was evening. The sun was obliterated by tremendous clouds, dark and heavy with rain, swelling in the colorless sky. As she rounded the final bend in the road and caught sight of Cedar Crest, Miranda saw that long shadows were bearing down on the mansion.

She was startled by its ominous appearance. She'd begun thinking of this place as a sanctuary.

Tonight—as with the night after she'd escaped the three horsemen—it was forbidding.

She fought the temptation to flee.

Go back, an inner voice warned. *You don't belong here.*

Yet she went on. Her desperation drove her forward. She rode furiously up to the front door and dropped her bike in the circular driveway. A raw wind had come up. Overhead, the dark clouds lumbered across the sky.

Go back.

"Garth?" she called. Her voice vanished into the wind.

The door to Cedar Crest opened, beckoning her inside.

Standing in the doorway, Miranda realized that the chill wind was emanating from the mansion, its icy gusts blowing out the door.

Placing her hand on the door frame to steady herself, she found that the wood was icy cold. Quickly she snatched her hand away.

"Garth?"

This time her tone was pleading. There was no response but the loud rumble of thunder.

Tentatively she stepped inside.

Cedar Crest was dark. The storm that was brewing had cast the interior in shadows. A sudden flash of lightning illuminated the entryway. And then, once again, the house remained cloaked in darkness.

A lone candle had been lit. It sat flickering, threatening to be blown out by the wind, on a small table in the front hall. She picked it up, clutching the brass candlestick firmly, protecting the fragile flame with her hand.

Slowly she began to walk.

The cavernous rooms of Cedar Crest, once welcoming, looked foreign to her. The dim light of the single candle did little to combat the deepening darkness. It cast grotesque shadows on the walls. Again and again she started at the unexpected sight of her own silhouette, magnified and looming ahead on a wall. Turning into a corridor, she gasped at her glaring reflection in a gilt-framed mirror.

The house felt empty. She knew now that Garth was not here. Yet she kept on, still parading through the desolate mansion, walking as if she were carrying out some mission she was determined to complete.

Go back.

The voice inside her head continued to warn her. Stubbornly Miranda resisted, paying it no heed.

And then she found herself in a bedroom at the end of a long corridor.

Garth's room. His possessions were scattered about and Miranda could almost feel his presence. She sat on the edge of his unmade bed, caressing the tangle of sheets and blankets that lay at the foot. She could smell his subtle scent, still lingering in the room. And the warmth from his body as he'd slept, hours earlier, seemed to emanate from the bedclothes.

A loud crack of thunder snapped her out of her dreamy state.

Why am I here? she wondered.

Almost as if in response, a bolt of lightning flashed, illuminating the room. A door she hadn't noticed before caught her attention.

Slowly Miranda rose from the bed. Moving as if she were in a trance, she went over to the door.

Go back.

She hesitated, then turned the doorknob.

Holding the candle before her, she peered into what turned out to be a closet. It was empty except for a large wooden crate. The box was huge, more than four feet high. Setting the candle on the floor, Miranda tried to move it. She pulled on the side, calling up every ounce of strength she possessed. It wouldn't budge.

She was about to turn away when she had another idea. Reaching for the top, she discovered the lid had already been pried open. She lifted it with ease.

With great caution Miranda reached inside. Her searching fingers closed around something hard, an oddly shaped item she couldn't identify. She brought it out of the box, examining it in the candle's glimmering light.

It was a ceramic figurine. A young shepherd, dressed in the clothing of a much earlier time, stood holding a staff. At his feet were two timid lambs. Miranda stared at it for a long time. There was something in the boy's look that intrigued her. It wasn't only his eyes, so lifelike she had to remind herself they were made from clay and paint. What struck her even more was the special glint shining in them, a look that sent a chill down her spine.

She reached into the crate a second time. This time, she retrieved a small box, painted pink and decorated with gold leaf. An intricate design was carved into the wood. Miranda held it lovingly in her hand, admiring its fine craftsmanship. It was a beautiful piece. She wondered who it had belonged to.

Her interest piqued by what she'd found so far, she delved into the box once again. This time her probing fingers made contact with wads of stiff paper. Gently she pulled out a large bundle, something heavy that had been wrapped with care in layers of tissue.

She laid it on the bed. The candle, still on the floor, cast large shadows across the stark white walls. Miranda began peeling away the layers of tissue paper, her curiosity growing.

Finally she pulled off the last piece. She bent down, straining to see in the dim light. As she did, the candle's flame flickered, then went out.

A small cry escaped her lips. But it didn't take long for common sense to prevail. She moved toward the small table at the side of Garth's bed, feeling around until she found a box of matches. She relit the candle, then went back to the object on the bed.

Miranda gasped. It was a grotesque mask, its handiwork and design clearly Native American. The face, carved into wood, was so grossly distorted and so oddly painted in red and black that it was frightening.

It was much larger than a real human head. Its nose was beaklike, its wide mouth stretched back into a cruel grimace, revealing two rows of crooked teeth. Two holes carved into the top formed hollowed-out eyes. A shock of hair, part black and part red, jutted out from the top, hanging down over the forehead. Along the top there were also chicken feathers, dyed green and blue and brown, as well as twigs and bits of bark, all nailed to the wooden mask.

Miranda knew this mask was the embodiment of evil. Yet what struck her the most were the two protrusions fastened to either side. They were sharply pointed, painted a garish shade of orange.

Horns.

The mask filled Miranda with horror. It was not only its ugliness. Not only the threatening expression on its face. Not only the demon it was clearly meant to represent.

It was something else, something that went beyond the mere physicality of the mask. . . .

Quickly Miranda wrapped it back up in the tissue paper. She couldn't stand to look at it anymore. She put it back in the wooden crate in the closet.

There would be no more exploring, she decided. She should leave. Garth wasn't home, and she didn't belong at Cedar Crest.

She was about to close the closet door and make her way back down the long dark hallway when something caught her eye. A large, shadowy shape at the bottom, wedged between the wooden crate and the back wall. Curious, she bent down to see what it was. She reached out to touch it.

Immediately she knew. The softness that greeted her fingertips could mean only one thing.

The wolfskin.

Garth had kept it. It was still here, tucked away safely at Cedar Crest. Her heartbeat quickened.

Go back. . . .

Falling to her knees, Miranda reached for the wolfskin, slowly dragging it out. As she did, a cloth bag fell from its folds. She peeked inside. It contained the herbs, with their distinctive pungent smell.

Straining, she managed to pull the heavy animal skin into the middle of the room. Eagerly she pressed her face against its velvety softness. Running her fingers through the fur, she closed her eyes, throwing back her head to luxuriate in the sensation.

She knew she should leave. But the lure of staying was too great. In spite of logic, in spite of the warnings flashing through her mind, Miranda couldn't pull herself away.

Suddenly there was an ear-shattering crack of thunder, so powerful it caused the entire house to tremble. Flashes of lightning lit up the room.

The window flew open.

And then she knew. The call of the night was too strong. She could not resist. . . .

She did not want to resist.

Miranda tucked the bag of herbs into her pocket. Then she picked up the wolfskin, struggling under its formidable weight. Slowly she made her way down the hall, toward the ballroom. Stepping inside, she was greeted by more flashes of lightning. In the tremendous mirrors lining the wall, she saw her own reflection: a girl with determination in her dark eyes, her hair streaming out wildly behind her, clutching an animal skin so heavy it took all her strength to carry it.

She gave her own image only a glance before heading toward the French doors. She headed outside, into the darkness. A heavy rain had begun to fall, cutting through the blackened sky, drops of silver that reflected the light of the moon.

The wolfskin, pulled up over her shoulders, sheltered Miranda from the downpour. She grabbed a stick and, finding a clear spot in the garden, quickly drew two concentric circles in the wet dirt. Reaching into the bag, she took out a handful of the herbs and rubbed them briskly against her skin.

Go back. Go back. . . .

She stepped inside the smaller circle. Within moments she could feel the change coming upon her. The earth began to rumble. Loud shrieks burst forth from the forest that surrounded her. And everywhere were the strangely shaped shadows, their forms changing as with undulating movements they wove in and out of the trees around Cedar Crest.

Slowly she began to lose contact with the present. Miranda could feel herself slipping away.

Go back, Miranda.

She let out a low moan, throwing back her head as she felt her body begin to change.

And then Miranda was gone.

A newly formed creature, a powerful she-wolf, turned and ran, disappearing into the night.

About the Author

Cynthia Blair, author of books for both adult and young-adult readers, has published more than thirty novels. She grew up on Long Island, New York, and earned her B.A. from Bryn Mawr College. After four years of working in New York City, she began writing full time. She currently lives on Long Island where she, like Miranda, loves spending time outdoors.